# She Loves You

# Yeah, Yeah, Yeah

# She Loves You

## Yeah, Yeah, Yeah

### by Ann Hood

PENGUIN WORKSHOP

PENGUIN WORKSHOP
An Imprint of Penguin Random House LLC, New York

Text copyright © 2018 by Ann Hood. All rights reserved.
First published in hardcover in 2018 by Penguin Workshop.
This paperback edition published in 2019 by Penguin Workshop,
an imprint of Penguin Random House LLC, New York.
PENGUIN and PENGUIN WORKSHOP are trademarks of
Penguin Books Ltd, and the W colophon is a registered
trademark of Penguin Random House LLC.
Printed in the USA.

The text in this book is set in Mercury Text.

Visit us online at www.penguinrandomhouse.com.

The Library of Congress has catalogued the hardcover edition
under the following Control Number: 2018009665.

ISBN 9781524785123                    10 9 8 7 6 5 4 3 2 1

For Paul,
Of course

# Prologue

Here are things that have made me excited:

1.  The day I found a sand dollar on the beach, all perfect and fragile and white. I was three or four years old and digging in the sand with my little red shovel. I used to love to build sand castles, and I would sit on my yellow-and-white-striped beach blanket and dig, dropping all that sand into my blue pail. Mom and I liked doing the drip technique when we built sand castles, which was to fill paper cups with water and drizzle the water over the castles to make turrets and towers. And this one day, my

shovel hit something hard, so I put it down and started using my fingers instead, and I uncovered the sand dollar. I had never seen one before, but somehow I knew it was a rare and special thing. So special that I didn't even pick it up right away. I just stared down at it resting in the smooth sand. My heart was beating hard and my mouth went dry and carefully I picked it up and held it, all warm and delicate, in the palm of my hand.

2. On the first day of first grade the teacher, Mrs. Kenney, made us come up to the board one by one and write our names. I sat in my little chair at my little desk, nervous that somehow I would do it wrong. I knew how to write my name. Well, print it in big block letters. TRUDY MIXER. I liked the mountains of the *M* and the sword swipe of the *X* and the tricky forked *Y*. But I'd never

written it in front of so many people, on a blackboard. Poor Gwendolyn Zamborini was standing up there writing her name and it had so many letters and it was taking up so much space that she started to cry and had to sit back down. Doris Fish didn't know how to write anything except the *D*, and she made it backward and stomped back to her seat, defiant. Robert Flick cried, too, because he was confused about his name—it was of course Robert, but everybody except Mrs. Kenney called him Bobby, and that was what he knew how to write. Then it was my turn, after so many mistakes and failures. I was wearing a navy-blue jumper with two pockets shaped like gray kitten heads on the front and a navy-blue pucker shirt and red knee socks and brand-new shoes with red laces. And I walked up to that blackboard, holding my breath the entire way. The chalk felt heavy in my hand when I lifted it to write that *T* and then the *R* and then I was writing all of it, not too big and not too small, and excitement rose up in me, I swear I could feel it filling me so much I almost thought it might lift me up like a balloon.

3. Also first grade. We were handed books with a picture on the front of a little girl and a little boy and a spotted dog all looking over a white picket fence. These, Mrs. Kenney told us, were our reading books. The boy was named Dick and the girl was named Jane and the dog was named Spot and the book was called *We Look and See*. Days and days went by with Mrs. Kenney making us learn the vowels and the sounds the different letters made. *What does this have to do with reading?* I thought as I dutifully drew a ladder and put *a, e, i, o, u* on each rung, dangling *y* off the top. And then one

day, I remember how the trees outside the window were in full autumn splendor, the leaves scarlet and golden and orange, I was staring at *We Look and See* and somehow I knew—*I knew*—that the words said: *Look, Jane. Look, Dick. See funny Sally. Funny, funny Sally.* I was reading! Reading! I started to shout, "Mrs. Kenney! Mrs. Kenney! I can read!"

4. "Do you want to be my best friend?" Michelle whispered to me during recess one morning in second grade. Michelle had long blond hair and big blue eyes, and she knew things like all the state birds (Colorado: lark bunting; Ohio: cardinal; Delaware: blue hen chicken) and the names of the presidents in order (George Washington, John Adams, Thomas Jefferson, James Madison, all the way to our president, John F. Kennedy) and the birthstone for every month (December,

zircon, mine; June, pearl, hers). I knew things like that, too, but other things, like the astrological signs (Sagittarius, me; Gemini, her) and the state capitals (even the hard ones like Tallahassee, Florida, and Frankfort, Kentucky) and the Seven Wonders of the Ancient World (such as the Great Pyramid of Giza and the Hanging Gardens of Babylon). In other words, we were a perfect fit, Michelle and me. We both hated mushrooms—*too slimy!*—and put ketchup instead of mustard on our hot dogs and vinegar instead of ketchup on our french fries. We both liked the color purple best and turquoise second best. We were lunar twins, which meant our birthdays were exactly six months apart, and in fourth grade we would both have our golden birthdays, which was when your age—nine—was the same as your birth date—also nine! "Do you want to be my best friend?" Michelle whispered to me that day, and it was like when you put the last piece in a big puzzle and step back and see how perfect it is. "Yes," I whispered back. And then we were.

5. February 9, 1964. My father and I watched the Beatles on *The Ed Sullivan Show*.

6. Today. I'm on a bus to Providence where I'll get on another bus to Boston where I'll take a subway to Suffolk Downs where I'll see the Beatles. Live. In concert. I press my hand to my pocketbook where the tickets sit waiting and my excitement is so big that it overtakes all of the other most exciting moments of my life combined. I rest my forehead on the window and watch Rhode Island whizzing past me outside. Every single cell I have is full, like I'm expanding, filling, lifting, floating, flying.

# CHAPTER ONE

# Yesterday

On February 9, 1964—just two and a half years ago—the British Invasion began. That was the night the Beatles appeared for the first time on *The Ed Sullivan Show*. I had tonsillitis. My tonsils were causing me a lot of trouble that winter, and Doctor Cooper was considering taking them out, an idea I did not like at all. Getting your tonsils out meant going into the hospital and staying at least one night. It meant having ether, a sickeningly sweet-smelling drug that put you to sleep. This I knew from Rosemary Martindale, who had her tonsils out in second grade. "They put a mask over your nose and mouth and the ether starts pouring out and they tell you to count backward from one hundred and all you want to do is scream and rip that mask off but you can't because of the ether," she explained to the whole class when she came back to school two weeks later. "Then you wake up with the worst sore throat you've ever had because they've cut out your tonsils." I ask you: Who would want to do this?

My neighbor Theresa Mazzoni, who went to Catholic school, came over that February afternoon. I was lying on the couch eating grape Popsicles and worrying about ether.

**\* \* \***

"Do you know what tonight is?" Theresa asked me.

"Sunday?" I croaked, because my throat was too sore for me to talk normally.

She rolled her eyes. "Not just any Sunday, Trudy," she said. "Tonight the Beatles are going to be on *The Ed Sullivan Show* and your life is going to change forever." She paused. "Everyone in America's life is going to change forever," she added.

I didn't like how Theresa always knew more than I did. How did she find out this stuff? She was just a kid, like me, but somehow she knew things I didn't know. One day she said to me, "Supercalifragilisticexpialidocious," and I said, "What?" And she said it again, faster and all smug. I didn't know what she was talking about, but I understood it was important and that in no time everyone else would be saying *supercalifragilisticexpialidocious,* too, and if I knew what was good for me I'd learn how to say it, too.

So I asked her, "What are the Beatles?"

"Not what, Trudy. Who."

Theresa flopped on the chair across from me and raised four fingers. "John, Paul, George, and Ringo," she said, counting each one off. "They're from England. *Liverpool,*" she said dreamily. "I like John best," she added.

I repeated the names in my head. John. Paul. George . . .

"Ringo?" I asked.

Theresa grinned. "Because he wears lots and lots of rings. He's the drummer."

Ah! So they were a musical group. Since it was Sunday, I knew that the Beatles were going to be on *The Ed Sullivan Show*, because that's where musical groups appeared on Sunday nights.

"I'll come over and watch with you if you want," Theresa said.

I did.

**\* \* \***

My parents were skeptical.

"The *Beatles*?" Mom said, scrunching her face the way she did when something tasted bad. "Why the *Beatles*?"

"They're in today's *New York Times*," Dad said, and he laid the newspaper out on the kitchen table.

Mom and I looked at the picture Dad was pointing

to. In the background was a Pan Am plane and in front of it were four boys with shaggy hair: the Beatles. The caption said that three thousand fans waiting for them to arrive nearly caused a riot when they stepped off the plane and onto American soil.

"They need haircuts," Mom said, scrunching her face even more.

Without even hearing one note of a Beatles song, I—like every girl in America—was already 100 percent smitten by them.

By the time Theresa showed up to watch *The Ed Sullivan Show* that night, Dad had read me the entire *New York Times* article and we'd listened to WPRO radio until "I Want to Hold Your Hand" came on, which was almost right away, because the song was already number one. In fact, the DJ dedicated fifteen whole minutes just to Beatles songs, playing "She Loves You," "I Saw Her Standing There," and "All My Loving" without interruption.

Dad was tapping his fingers on the table in time

to the music. "Oh, Trudy," he said, "these guys are good."

"It's not very melodic, is it?" Mom said. Mom liked Frank Sinatra.

Dad's eyes met mine, and it was like he looked at me for the first time ever. No, like he *saw* me for the first time ever. We smiled at each other, two Beatles fans. Dad nodded, as if to say that we were in this together. I felt so happy, I almost forgot my sore throat.

"I like Paul best," I announced when Theresa showed up.

"So do I," Dad told her.

He scooped ice cream into bowls for us and set up the TV trays. Usually Mom did this stuff, but she wasn't a Beatles fan. She didn't understand.

Ed Sullivan announced, "Ladies and gentlemen, the Beatles," and the girls in the audience screamed and cried.

Theresa screamed, too. I couldn't, of course,

because of my tonsils. But it didn't even matter because there were the Beatles on the stage singing, and all I really wanted to do was sit there and watch them. I wanted them to never stop singing because somehow Theresa was right. The Beatles had arrived and everything changed.

Later, after the show was over and Theresa went home, Dad came and sat beside me on my bed.

"Last November we all lost hope, Trudy," he said softly.

I knew what he meant. The November before, on November 22 to be exact, Lee Harvey Oswald had shot and killed President Kennedy, and the whole country went into mourning. Our principal, Mrs. Abbott, ran into our classroom sobbing and said, "Our beloved president has been shot," and she told us all to go home. When I got home, my mother and Mrs. Mazzoni and all the other mothers from the neighborhood, except Mrs. Blaise because she worked as a nurse in the ER, were sitting in front of the TV, crying. That's how I knew for sure it was true.

Dad took my hand. "But the Beatles are bringing joy back into our hearts," he said, and he squeezed my hand. "I love you, yeah, yeah, yeah," he whispered, and kissed me on the forehead.

"I love you, too, Dad," I whispered back.

I closed my eyes, and the song played over and over in my mind, like a lullaby putting me to sleep.

**\* \* \***

The day I went back to school after my tonsils were healed, I stood up in class and announced the formation of the Beatles Fan Club.

"The first meeting is today, right after school," I said. "The sign-up sheet will be outside the office."

By lunchtime, fourteen kids had signed up. And I, Trudy Mixer, became the most popular girl at Robert E. Quinn Elementary.

# CHAPTER TWO

# A Hard Day's Night

Two years later, and I was still the straight-A student and president of the Robert E. Quinn *Junior High* Beatles Fan Club. With twenty-three members, it was the most popular after-school club at Quinn. More popular even than Future Teachers (eleven members), Make America Beautiful (ten, which is shocking, because all they did was pick up litter), and Future Cheerleaders (nine). Then I came back from April vacation and everything changed.

Of course, everything always seemed to be changing in the outside world—like boys were growing their hair as long as girls, and people were protesting the war in Vietnam instead of, as Dad said, "just going to fight over there and protect democracy," and everyone was complaining about President Johnson. But things on the inside world—my world—had been the same for as long as I could remember. I was president of the fan club. Michelle was my best friend. Teachers called me a natural-born leader and good citizen. But all of that changed when I walked into second period, social studies, on the first day back from vacation.

Instead of our teacher, Mr. Flora, there was a substitute teacher, a woman with short dark hair, cat glasses, a dress with a big curlicue *P* on the left side, and a sour face that stared out at us like we were Martians. On the board she had written her name: Mrs. Peabody. Apparently Mr. Flora had to have emergency surgery over the break and he would not be recovered enough to return to school. This Mrs. Peabody announced in a matter-of-fact way, but we all got very nervous.

"What kind of surgery?" Dennis Dannon asked.

"My mother had her appendix out but she got better in like three weeks," Mary Beth Argo said.

Poor Mr. Flora! We were all really upset because he was one of our favorite teachers, a bald round man who wore bow ties.

"Is he going to die?" someone in the back of the room shouted, and we all gasped.

"Okay, people," Mrs. Peabody said, "settle down."

Settling down thirty-one sixth-graders took a very long time, so when I couldn't catch Michelle's eye, I sighed and stared out the window.

Outside, it looked like the world had just woken up after a long sleep. The trees were bursting with bright green buds, and the first daffodils had poked their heads out of the dirt. Staring out the window instead of at Mrs. Peabody, a Beatles song kind of drifted across my brain, which was typical, because unless I was doing math or reading a book or memorizing facts, I was usually thinking about the Beatles. On this particular day the song that I was hearing was "In My Life," probably because the night before, I'd played the album *Rubber Soul* about a million times waiting for Michelle to call me. Which she never did, I remembered, and the same feeling of unease that I had all last night rose up again. Come to think of it, I realized as I stared out at those trees, I'd only seen Michelle once over all of vacation, which was very weird.

I made myself think of "In My Life," saying the words in my head, *There are places I remember, all my life, though some have changed* . . . And eventually my thoughts turned to Paul McCartney, all the way across the Atlantic Ocean in England, maybe writing a new song at this very moment.

Clearly I had been daydreaming for quite a while, because when I looked away from the window, Mrs. Peabody was pointing to a map of ancient Rome that hung from the blackboard and telling us in a very excited voice how by June we would be able to name all of the Roman emperors and recite Marc Antony's eulogy for Julius Caesar. I tried to catch Michelle's eye again, but she was staring at that map as if it held the secret to something. Kenny Prescott, the boy with the best swoop of bangs falling into his eyes and also the longest eyelashes, was looking at me and not in a good way, so I stared at the map, too, sounding out the names in my head. Macedonia. Cappadocia. Mesopotamia.

"So," Mrs. Peabody said, "let's see who's coming to ancient Rome with me!"

She picked up the attendance book and started at the top.

"Mary Beth Argo?"

"Here," Mary Beth said in her timid little voice. She still played with dolls, in particular Little Kiddles, the tiny dolls with long hair that came in plastic perfume bottles or fancy egg-shaped containers. Mary Beth kept them in her desk, and when she got bored, which was almost always, she took them out and combed their hair with her fingers.

"Nora Goldsmith?"

"Here," Nora said. Her eyes were all red and puffy, like she'd been crying.

But Mrs. Peabody didn't seem to notice, she just kept calling out our names, her companions into ancient Rome. I wondered if Paul McCartney had studied ancient Rome. I knew his junior high in Liverpool was called the Joseph Williams Junior School and he went there after the Stockton Wood Road Primary School in Liverpool. I knew that Paul was one of only four kids out of ninety who passed the 11-plus exam and gained admission to the Liverpool Institute, an all-boys grammar school, which is what they call high school in England, with an excellent academic reputation. I knew he got As in art and English and geography. Basically, I knew everything about Paul McCartney.

Mrs. Peabody's voice interrupted my thinking about Paul McCartney. "Gertrude Mixer," she said.

I froze.

"Gertrude Mixer," she said again, louder this time.

Someone giggled.

A boy from somewhere behind me said, "Gertrude," like he was calling a cat.

Michelle tilted her blond head in my direction and looked at me like she was seeing me for the very first time. I loved Michelle because she was my best friend, but I had to admit that ever since the Beatles song "Michelle" came out last year she could be a little full of herself. Sometimes she even threw French words in normal conversation, just because the song did: *Sont les mots qui vont très bien ensemble* . . . Sometimes when I played *Rubber Soul*, I skipped the song "Michelle" and went straight to "It's Only Love." For example, like last night when Michelle didn't call me.

"Gertrude!" Mrs. Peabody practically shouted.

Her eyes scanned the room, searching for the owner of that horrible, old lady, old-fashioned, ugly name.

I wanted to disappear. But that was not an option. Every single kid was looking straight at me, waiting.

Slowly, I raised my hand.

"Here," I squeaked.

Until that moment, I had been Trudy Mixer, straight-A student and president of the Robert E. Quinn Junior High Beatles Fan Club. Suddenly, I realized, I was now Gertrude. *Ger-trude*. Suddenly, I realized with, as Dad says when he realizes something important, "stunning clarity," my life as I knew it was over.

I liked to get to the Beatles Fan Club meetings early so I could write a new Fab Four Fun Fact on the blackboard and organize the mimeographed quizzes and the fan letter envelopes. We met every Wednesday after school in Mr. Bing's science lab,

a room that smelled like formaldehyde and BO—
formaldehyde because that's where the frogs got
dissected, and BO because it was a ninth-grade
classroom and ninth-grade boys had BO.

On this Wednesday, the very day that Mrs.
Peabody had turned me from Trudy into Gertrude,
Mr. Bing had already left for the day. For this, I was
relieved. Not only did it give me time to get organized, but it also allowed me to briefly go over all
the ways my day had gone wrong ever since social
studies. For one thing, Michelle had sat with Becky
Thorpe and Kimberly Franklin during lunch.
Instead of with me. I'd hovered by their table a
moment, and even though Becky had smiled at
me—with *pity*—I thought, Michelle had basically
ignored me. She was drinking her eggnog-flavored
Carnation Instant Breakfast from the little cup
that came with her thermos, in an effort to lose
ten pounds and be as skinny as the model Twiggy,
The Face of 1966.

While I stood there being awkward, Michelle told Becky and Kimberly that she was going to get her hair cut as short as Twiggy's, and they both gasped. No one at Quinn had short hair. We all wore our hair exactly the same way—long, straight, and parted down the middle—except for poor Angela Silva, who was cursed with curly hair. Even when she ironed it, in no time her curls sprung right back.

"You're cutting your hair?" I blurted. "Since when?"

Michelle glanced up at me, barely, then just kept on talking like I wasn't standing there holding a tray with a sloppy joe and an apple on it.

"Michelle?" I said, trying to make my voice sound strong and confident. "When did you decide that?"

Michelle sighed. "I don't know, Trudy. Over break."

The one time we had seen each other over April

break, Michelle had most definitely not mentioned cutting her hair as short as Twiggy's.

Becky said, "Do you want to sit with us?"

I didn't. I wanted Michelle to get up and for the two of us to find seats together somewhere. But that was obviously not going to happen. So I said *Sure* and sat down across from Michelle and ate my sloppy joe while they all talked about how *The Sound of Music* was the best movie they'd ever seen. Apparently, they had all gone to see it together over break.

"Didn't you love the part where Maria makes them the matching outfits out of curtains?" Becky asked me.

I had not yet seen *The Sound of Music*, so I had no idea who Maria was or who she made outfits of curtains for.

"Yeah," I said. "I love that part."

✻ ✻ ✻

Also, for the rest of that day, whenever I changed

classes, the boys whispered, *Ger-trude*, all creepy-like as I walked by.

Then last period, French class, Mr. Lamereaux assigned us French names for when we had practice conversations, except of course Michelle, whose name was already French. Every girl had a crush on Mr. Lamereaux: He drove a red convertible MG and he looked like Herman from the group Herman's Hermits.

Mary Beth's French name was Bijoux, which meant "little jewel," and Becky got Babette and Kimberly got Camille and Nora—still with her red eyes—got Desirée and Jessica, the least popular girl in the entire grade if not the entire school, got the beautiful name Mirabelle.

"Ah, Mademoiselle Mixer," Mr. Lamereaux said to me, "your French name is . . ."

I was so excited I couldn't sit still. Oceane? Emanuelle? Delphine?

A slow smile crept across Mr. Lamereaux's face.

"Why, like Michelle my belle, *you* already have a French name, too!"

I swallowed hard. "I do?"

For the second time that day, a teacher said that old-fashioned, old-lady, ugly name right out loud. In front of everyone. It didn't help that Mr. Lamereaux pronounced the *G* like a *J*, the way they do in French.

"Gertrude," he said.

**\* \* \***

Clutching the still warm mimeos to my chest in the science lab, I could practically still hear the class laughing. *Jer-trude!* I pressed the paper to my nose, inhaling the delicious inky smell.

Well, I told myself, in six minutes twenty-three Beatles Fan Club members are going to walk in this room and you, Trudy Mixer, will once again be in charge, on top of the world. I put the quizzes on Mr. Bing's desk, next to his weird collection of troll dolls. Then I picked up a fat piece of purple chalk (purple was George's favorite color, one of the quiz questions today) and wrote the Fab Four Fun Fact of the Day on the board:

> John Lennon's middle name, Winston, was given to him as an act of wartime patriotism to honor then prime minister Winston Churchill.

I stepped back and admired my handwriting, and the fun fact itself.

The door opened and in walked Peter Haywood, the lone boy in the fan club.

"Hi, Trudy," he said, and I could have hugged him for not calling me Gertrude.

"Hi," I said.

"Do you know what onomatopoeia is?" he asked me. His cheeks were bright red when he asked me, and his cowlick trembled a little.

"Yes," I said, even though I didn't. I just hated not knowing something.

Peter grinned and turned even redder. Candy apples came to mind.

"What's your favorite example of onomatopoeia?" he asked me.

Peter's eyes are a color called hazel, which is kind of golden, which is strange for eyes. This close I could see that there was some green in them, too. And maybe a little brown ring around the pupil.

"It's a combination of Rayleigh scattering and melanin," Peter said.

At first I thought he was explaining this onomato thing, but then he said, "Rayleigh scattering is what makes the sky look blue, and melanin is the pigment that makes brown eyes brown."

Then I knew he was explaining hazel eyes.

"Huh," I said, because what else could I say to such a weird thing? Besides, I didn't like how he knew I was practically gazing into his eyes.

"Most people with hazel eyes are water signs," Peter said.

"Are you?"

"I'm a Cancer. July seventh."

"That's Ringo's birthday!" I said.

"I know," he said. "I'm in the fan club, remember?"

The fan club.

I frowned and looked at the clock. 3:21. Everyone except Peter was six minutes late.

"*Chug, chug, chug. Puff, puff, puff. Ding-dong, ding-dong.* The little train rumbled over the tracks."

"What?" I said, not trying to hide how annoyed I was. What was he talking about? And where was everyone?

"*The Little Engine That Could!*" Peter said, as if that explained anything.

The door opened again and weird Jessica Mancini skulked in, followed by Nora Goldsmith.

Peter didn't seem to notice. "That's my favorite example of onomatopoeia!" he said proudly.

Nora smiled, maybe for the first time that day.

*"Well, my heart went boom, when I crossed that room—"* she sang from "I Saw Her Standing There," one of my all-time favorite Beatles songs, even though it was the flip side of "I Want to Hold Your Hand." I considered telling these three this Fab Four Fact, but Peter was already talking, telling Nora what a good example of onomatopoeia that was.

Apparently everyone knew about this onomato thing. Except me. Which made me very cranky. Also: Um, where was everyone?

"I guess we'll wait a few more minutes," I said, trying to sound like someone in charge.

"Michelle's not coming," Jessica said. "She went to Future Cheerleaders."

"Michelle?" I repeated, just in case my hearing had suddenly gone bad. "Future Cheerleaders?"

"With Becky and Kimberly," Jessica added.

Now my heart was going boom, but not in a good

way like in the song. So that's what onomato was—words that sounded like a sound. *Boom*.

At 3:30 Nora said, "If we don't start I'm going to miss the late bus."

"Okay," I said, even though my brain was saying FutureCheerleadersFutureCheerleaders over and over.

I handed out the quizzes, printed in smudged purple mimeograph ink. From somewhere in the distance I heard voices rise, calling, "Give me a *Q*!"

Jessica rolled her eyes. "Cheerleaders," she said under her breath.

By the time everyone finished the quiz and I read off the right answers, it was almost four o'clock and we hadn't even written our fan letter begging the Beatles to come to Boston for another concert.

"We could write them when we get home," Peter offered.

"No we can't," I said. "It's a club activity."

The twenty-three envelopes, already stamped

and addressed, seemed to mock me. Twenty-three fan club letters might help to persuade the Beatles to give a concert in Boston. But *four* letters? Four letters couldn't convince anyone to do anything.

Nora was buttoning her jacket. "The bus," she said apologetically.

And just like that, the members of the Robert E. Quinn Junior High Beatles Fan Club all made their way to the door.

Peter turned. "Bye," he said.

I didn't answer. I couldn't. My Beatles Fan Club had dwindled to almost nothing.

"What's that spell?" the cheerleaders yelled. "Quinn!"

I could almost swear I heard Michelle yelling louder than anyone.

# CHAPTER THREE

# All My Loving

On February 9, 1964, the Beatles appeared on *The Ed Sullivan Show*. The next day, February 10, I formed the first Beatles Fan Club in the entire state of Rhode Island. I even got an official certificate from the Beatles Fan Club Headquarters in Liverpool stating that mine was the original Rhode Island chapter. For the rest of that year, we met every week, playing Beatles records and making big buttons with our favorite Beatle's face on them. Most kids liked John or Paul. Michelle had the biggest crush on John, even though under his name on *The Ed Sullivan Show* it said: SORRY GIRLS,

HE'S MARRIED. "He's smart and sarcastic and he's a poet," she said. "Besides, his wife is so cool." Nora chose Ringo, claiming he was the best drummer who'd ever lived. Also, she said he had a twinkle in his eye. No one wanted George, so I made Jessica wear a George pin because she was the kind of person who George would like: quiet and kind of weird. *Say quirky, not weird,* my mother always told me. But Jessica wasn't quirky. She was weird.

Me, I love Paul. Last year when Paul sang "Yesterday" alone on *The Ed Sullivan Show,* I almost fainted. I got all light-headed and tingly and I couldn't move, not even my pinky. It was like he hypnotized me or something. This was one of my favorite Fab Four Fun Facts:

> *Did you know that one morning Paul woke up with a lovely melody in his head and went straight to the piano to play it? But the only lyrics he could think of were*

*"Scrambled eggs, oh my baby how I love your legs . . ." That song became the hit "Yesterday"!!!*

That was the first Fab Four Fun Fact, but honestly, I could have added so much more. Like how Paul was living in London, on Wimpole Street, with his girlfriend Jane Asher's family. Or how the lyrics finally came to him when he and Jane Asher were driving to Portugal. Or that "Yesterday" was the first song Paul wrote without John, even though the record says Lennon-McCartney. The one time I saw her over April break, Michelle told me that my love of the Beatles was getting out of hand.

"I mean really, Trudy," she said, "you know Jane Asher's address? Don't you think that's kind of, I don't know, crazy?"

"It's in all the fan magazines," I said. "Everybody knows it."

I didn't tell her that I also knew Jane Asher's birthday and her parents' names and a million other things. I didn't want my best friend to think I was crazy. Besides, didn't she love all kinds of facts, too (152 breeds of dogs, all the countries below the equator, the names of every First Lady from Martha to Lady Bird)? Also, I just loved the Beatles. And everything about the Beatles. Especially Paul. Which is why on the way home from school after the lowest-attended, worst meeting ever of the Beatles Fan Club, I decided I had to do something big. Something extraordinary. Something that would return me to my rightful place in the suddenly terrible, confusing world of the sixth grade.

I had to do something. But what?

*  *  *

"How was school?" Mom asked me that night at dinner, which was meat loaf, my least favorite thing in the world.

I poured practically a whole bottle of ketchup on it to hide the meat loaf taste.

"Honestly, Trudy," Mom said, shaking her head.

Dad didn't notice. He was too busy reading the *Wall Street Journal*, his face hidden behind it. Lately, he read the newspaper every night during dinner because he claimed it was beneficial to always do more than one thing at a time. For example, when he watched TV he also ate celery because all that chewing actually burned calories, and when he drove he recited things like the Gettysburg Address or the Bill of Rights to keep his mind alert. But even if he wasn't reading the newspaper or reciting the Gettysburg Address, Dad did not pay very much attention to me. To anyone really. Except his job. Mostly, he looked at me like I was someone vaguely familiar.

Mom always reminded me when I complained about Dad ignoring me that Dad has a *big important job* that kept him preoccupied, even when he was home. He has one of those jobs without a real name and that's too complicated to explain. Every now and then he would glance in our direction and say something from the newspaper that we didn't understand, like: *Do you think it would be a good idea for music to play in elevators and grocery stores?*

That was the question he asked over meat loaf that night.

"Charles"—Mom laughed—"why would someone play music in an elevator?"

"What kind of music?" I asked.

"Soft music. Nonintrusive music. Music you don't notice."

Mom laughed even harder. "If you don't notice it, why do you need it?"

But he was back behind the paper again, lost to us.

Mom and I chewed our peas. She made a little hill out of her mashed potatoes. Dad turned the page.

"I would like Beatles music to play in elevators," I said. "And grocery stores. And maybe even just in the air so that when I'm walking to school I could hear 'I Saw Her Standing There.'"

The *Wall Street Journal* dipped slightly and the top of Dad's face appeared.

"Now there's a good idea, Trudy," he said. "Beatles music in the grocery store."

I thought I might burst. Dad had paid attention! To me! I had a good idea!

"Dad, did you know Paul wrote that song for Jane Asher?" I said, hearing how hard I was trying. "'I Saw Her Standing There'?"

Mom cleared her throat. "Now who's Jane Asher? The actress in that movie I liked? With the red hair?"

"She's only Paul McCartney's girlfriend," I muttered.

"Charles, what was that movie?" she said brightly.

Dad speared a chunk of meat loaf and brought it to his mouth.

"How can you eat meat loaf without ketchup?" I asked him.

Nothing.

"Hello? Dad? Remember me? Trudy?"

He peeked from around the paper, his eyes soft. "Of course I do. You're that girl who loves the Beatles." Then he was gone again. I smiled.

Mom cocked her head. "I think it has the word *masque* in the title," she said.

I sighed. *"The Masque of the Red Death,"* I told her.

"Right! With Vincent Price and this Jane Asher person you're talking about." Mom nodded. "It was very good. Scary."

Dad folded up the *Wall Street Journal*, not all messy, like when Mom folds a newspaper, but right on the creases. He got up and looked around like he was trying to remember where he was. Then he said, "Great meat loaf, Kay," and wandered off. We heard the door of his study close and we knew we wouldn't be seeing him again tonight.

"Today was the worst day I've ever had in school in my entire life," I said.

Mom had started to clear the table, but she stopped, the bowl of peas in one hand and the platter of meat loaf in the other.

"Worse than the day you broke your tooth on the water fountain?" she asked.

"Yes."

"Worse than the day you threw up on Kenny Prescott?"

"Mom. Today was the worst day ever," I said.

She sat back down. "What happened, sweetie?"

I looked at her mom face, pretty but not perfect, surrounded by a cloud of ash-blond hair stiff as meringue. She always wore pale pink lipstick and Arpège perfume and matching sweater sets. In other words, she looked like a mom from a

TV show. She was sitting there, waiting with her Worried Mom face, but I couldn't explain why the day had been so awful.

"Well, we got a new social studies teacher," I began slowly. "Mr. Flora had to have emergency surgery."

"Oh dear," she said.

"I hate the new teacher," I said. "Mrs. Peabody."

Everything that happened started to roil around in my stomach. *Ger-trude* and Michelle with Becky and Kim at lunch and getting the worst French name and then only three kids—three! And the worst three in the whole grade—coming to the Beatles Fan Club meeting, all of it mixed up inside me with the taste of meat loaf and ketchup.

"I think I'm going to be sick," I said.

And just like that, Mom put down the peas and the meat loaf and appeared with a big pot for me to throw up in.

But I didn't throw up.

Instead I had that thought again: I need to do something big.

Then I had another thought: I need to meet Paul McCartney.

I looked at Mom and smiled.

"You're not going to throw up?" she said.

"Nope."

She placed the back of her hand on my forehead. "You're cool as a cucumber," she announced. "Come on, let's clean up so we can watch *The Beverly Hillbillies.*"

That was her way of helping me feel better. She hated *The Beverly Hillbillies,* which was a show about the Clampett family who were hillbillies from Kentucky who discovered oil and got rich and moved to Beverly Hills where they embarrassed themselves in silly ways. "No one is that dumb," she'd say when Jethro or Jed did something stupid. She liked a show called *The Monroes,* which was a western about five orphans trying to survive as a family on the frontier. "That Barbara Hershey is so pretty," Mom always said whenever Barbara Hershey appeared on the screen.

"That's okay, Mom," I said. "I have a project to work on."

She looked at me, surprised. "You're going to pass up *The Beverly Hillbillies*? And possibly some popcorn?"

"Thanks," I said. "But I need to get started on an idea I have."

I tried to help her clean up, but she shooed me away.

"I can do it in no time," she said.

She put on the radio to her station, the one that played singers like Vic Damone and Dean Martin and Frank Sinatra. The worst radio station of all the radio stations. Then she filled the sink with hot water and dish detergent. Some song came on that I didn't recognize, but Mom started singing along with it right away. *All summer long we sang a song and then we strolled that golden sand, Two sweethearts and the summer wind . . .*

I groaned. So sappy.

I went in my room and closed the door. I could still hear Mom, but only a little. My bedroom was all white—bed, bureau, night table, desk—with gold trim and mint-green-and-white dotted swiss curtains and bedspread. I hated it. I wanted mod furniture and the Marimekko sheets with the giant red and orange flowers on them like I saw in *Seventeen* magazine. But Mom refused, because classics last forever and trends do not. She did get me a director's chair with my name on it, but I had to practically beg for it.

I sat in that chair at the white desk and opened my favorite notebook. On the cover were silhouettes of a boy and girl walking on the beach and the paper inside was purple. I turned to a blank page and wrote:

*Ways to Meet Paul McCartney:*

1. *Go to his house in St. John's Wood in London and wait for him to come out.*

2. *Write to the Beatles' manager, Brian Epstein, and request a meeting with Paul.*

3. *Um . . .*

There was no number three. I either had to go all the way to London or hope that Brian Epstein would understand how vital meeting Paul McCartney was to my survival and set up a meeting, preferably here in Rhode Island. These options seemed grim. Futile. Hopeless even.

It was at times like this that Michelle could make me laugh. She could say just one thing, like *Mary Land,* because in third grade I thought that was how you said the name of the state

Maryland. Or *mi-sled*, because in fourth grade when Michelle had to read out loud she pronounced the word *misled* as *mi-sled*. We had about a million things like that, and I decided that Michelle was just the thing I needed, even though I was mad at her.

I went into the living room to get the telephone and there was Mom watching *The Monroes*.

She pointed to the screen. "Isn't that Barbara Hershey the prettiest thing?" she said.

"Yup," I said, and carried the telephone into the hallway, stretching its cord as far as it would go. Then I dialed Michelle's number by heart.

"Hello?" she answered, sounding eager.

"Hi," I said. "It's me. Trudy."

"I know it's you," she said.

"Well, I didn't want you to be mi-sled."

She didn't actually laugh. She more like snorted.

"I hate Mrs. Peabody," I said.

"She's all right, I guess."

"What kind of emergency surgery do you think Mr. Flora had?"

"I don't know. Becky thinks it was a heart thing," Michelle said.

I frowned. *Becky*.

"But Kim heard it was a hip replacement."

*Kim*.

"Oh!" I said. "You forgot to come to the Beatles Fan Club meeting today." For some reason, my throat felt like I had something stuck in it.

"I didn't forget," Michelle said softly. "I dropped out."

"Of the fan club?" I asked her stupidly, because it was just impossible to believe.

"I joined Future Cheerleaders," Michelle said. "It was so cool. We're going to learn how to do cartwheels and splits and everything."

"But we think cheerleading is dumb," I reminded her.

"Well, I don't think that. Not anymore. It's really

fun." Then she added, "Becky can already do a split."

"That's not so hard," I said, even though I had no idea how a person could do a split without breaking something, like a leg.

For the first time maybe ever, Michelle and I sat in silence. Almost silence anyway; I could hear her breathing.

"Well," she said after a million years went by, "I have to go. I'm expecting a call."

"Oh," I said, and then we didn't say anything for another million years.

"We're getting uniforms," Michelle said finally. "Pleated skirts and sweaters with a big *Q* on them."

"I'm going to meet Paul McCartney."

"Trudy," she said, and I knew if I could see through the phone all the way to her house I would see her rolling her big blue eyes.

"I am."

"No you're not, Trudy," she said.

"I'm serious," I said, maybe trying to keep her on the phone.

"How in the world can a kid from Rhode Island meet one of the most famous people in the whole world, Trudy? I mean, he's a Beatle. Kids don't meet Beatles."

"You can come with me," I said.

"Oh Trudy," Michelle said, and she hung up.

Just then the door to my father's study opened and he came out, holding his briefcase.

He walked down the hall, right toward me, and as he approached I said, "Guess what, Dad?"

"Not now, Trudy. I have to call Peterson."

Dad always had to call Peterson, some guy in his office who did the same mysterious stuff Dad did.

I watched him walk all the way to the living room and then back.

"I need the telephone," he said, holding out his hand.

Once he had the phone, he dialed standing right there in the hall.

"Peterson," he said into it, "Mixer."

He shot me his *Give Me Some Privacy* look.

"I'm going to meet Paul McCartney," I said.

But he wasn't paying attention.

*** 

Things I love about Dad:

1.  Piggyback rides

2.  How he taught me to tie my shoes with a poem: *Bunny ears, Bunny ears, playing by a tree. Crisscrossed the tree, trying to catch me. Bunny ears, Bunny ears, jumped into the hole. Popped out the other side, beautiful and bold!* And even though that was back when I was five, sometimes when I'm tying my shoes even now I can hear him reciting that poem to me.

3.  Before he got his big promotion and he didn't have to work all the time, he used to

make me pancakes that looked like Mickey Mouse—one big pancake for the face and then two little ones for the mouse ears. Sometimes he still does it, just not a lot, because he always has to be on the phone with Peterson or read up on technology things or write memos and letters and reports.

4. I used to think he turned the lights on and off by magic. When I got older and realized he was bumping the switch up and down with his shoulder, I didn't even care. It still felt like magic.

5. Facts. A lot of facts. He knows almost everything. In a good way.

6. He knows how to sail and on warm summer nights sometimes he takes me with him to the East Greenwich Yacht Club, which sounds fancy but is not fancy at all, and takes me out sailing on a Sunfish.

7.  And sometimes he tips us over on purpose, which is almost more fun than the sailing part.

8.  When he dances in the kitchen with my mother, he sings along with Frank Sinatra, right in Mom's ear, and she closes her eyes and smiles.

9.  Also when he dances with me in the kitchen, I stand on his size 12 feet and he moves me across the floor like that.

10. The Beatles, obviously.

# CHAPTER FOUR

# From Me to You

Fab Four Fun Fact of the Day:

> Or should I say Fab Five??? Stuart Sutcliffe has been called the "Fifth Beatle." He was the original bassist of the five-member band. Instead of replacing him when he died of a brain hemorrhage, Paul McCartney changed from rhythm guitar to bass. While Sutcliffe was mainly in the band because he was friends with Lennon, he was the first to wear the Beatles' famous "mop top" hairstyle.

I stepped back and admired my Fun Fact. It was a good one—historical, complex, informative.

"Seriously?" Jessica said when she walked in to the Fan Club meeting. "Everyone on the planet knows about Stuart Sutcliffe."

"Maybe everyone on the planet knows about Stuart, but there's a lot of information here."

Jessica shrugged and sat down.

If I didn't have a big white envelope from London, England, waiting in my bag, I might have gotten angry. But today was going to be the best day of my life, so I wasn't going to let Jessica ruin it.

She was actually wearing a Girl Scout uniform. In sixth grade. That was maybe the most embarrassing, least cool thing a person could do. But there she sat in her too-long green dress and bright yellow bow around her neck and a sash filled with merit badges. I glanced down. Yup. She had on green knee socks, too. I groaned inwardly. Who would have ever thought that I, Trudy Mixer, would be stuck with Jessica Mancini, one-quarter of the Beatles Fan Club?

Since our very first meeting, our membership had stayed at exactly twenty-four, counting me, the president. But now we were the after-school club with the *fewest* members, one less than the newly formed Sixth-Graders Against the Vietnam War. All they did was wear black armbands and make posters with pop letters that said things like MAKE LOVE, NOT WAR. At least we actually did things.

Nora came in, looking all worried. I sighed. Nora *and* Jessica, two of the least popular girls in the entire school. Nora always looked unkempt. Her hems were raggedy, her hair was tangled, and she smelled sour, like her clothes hadn't been washed. Today she had on a poor boy shirt that was at least one size too small, but it had in fact been washed— with something red, because that white shirt was now an uneven pink.

Nora was frowning at the Fun Fact, too. "I wish this club did something," she said.

"What do you mean?" I said. "We do lots of things."

"All we do is play records and write fan letters. It's getting kind of boring," Nora said. "My mother says that if I don't spend my after-school time more wisely then I have to come right home."

By now Peter had come in, too, his cowlicks sticking up and his shirt untucked. Last year this room had been packed for every meeting. Packed with the best kids in fifth grade. Sure, Jessica and Nora and Peter had been there, too, but I'd hardly noticed them in the crowd. Now all I could do was notice them.

"Last week we analyzed the words to 'Nowhere Man'!" I reminded Nora. "That was complicated. And important."

I was desperate. If Nora dropped out of the club, we wouldn't be a club anymore. School rules said that a club needs at least four people to be approved.

"I don't know," Jessica said. Even though it was almost May, it was still cold, and she had on a short-sleeve shirt. No jacket.

"I think analyzing the words to 'Nowhere Man' will help us prepare for our poetry section in English," Peter said.

Jessica chewed on her bottom lip.

"The song is about loneliness," Peter continued. *"He's a real nowhere man, Sitting in his nowhere land, Making all his nowhere plans for nobody . . ."*

*"Isn't he a bit like you and me?"* I said, and I grinned at Peter, who immediately blushed.

"It's just that my mother is so strict. And she likes me to be home. With her," Nora said, and I almost thought she was going to cry.

I cleared my throat.

"Well, I wanted to close the meeting with this, but I guess I should do it now instead." I opened my macramé bag and pulled out a big envelope. It had an airmail stamp on it, and the return address said London, England. The envelope had arrived yesterday, and it took all my willpower not to open it. But I decided that the Beatles Fan Club should share the excitement.

"Is that from England?" Nora said, her eyes wide.

I nodded.

"Three weeks ago I wrote a letter to Brian Epstein—"

"The Beatles' manager Brian Epstein?" Nora said, her eyes even wider.

"The one and only," I said. "I wrote to him and asked him if he could arrange a meeting with me and Paul McCartney."

"Oh, Trudy," Jessica said, sounding very much like Michelle had on the phone.

"Jessica," I said, "do you think a letter saying that was impossible would come in such a big envelope?"

"I don't know," Jessica said.

"Letters that say no come in regular legal envelopes," I said. My father had told me that once, and I believed him because he knew stuff like that. "Letters that say yes come in envelopes like this."

"Do you think Brian Epstein is going to fly you somewhere to meet Paul?" Peter asked.

That was exactly what I thought. Even though I hadn't opened the envelope, I'd examined it and I could tell there was something besides a letter inside.

"I just read their tour schedule in *Tiger Beat*," Nora said. "They're playing Germany and Japan! You might be going to Tokyo!"

"Personally," I said, "I think it's for their May first concert in London."

"Are you going to go to Carnaby Street, too?" Nora gushed.

"I'll bring back souvenirs from there," I said.

"Are you going to meet Jane Asher?" Jessica asked.

I said, "I hope so!"

Peter looked worried. "Maybe you should open it," he said. "Before you make too many plans."

You know how on Christmas morning you race to the tree to open all your presents, but then once you get there you kind of dillydally? Like the suspense is almost better than the presents themselves? That was how I felt in that moment. That envelope held the key to my future. After I met Paul McCartney, the fan club membership would skyrocket. I'd be like a celebrity, not just in school but also in the whole town. Maybe even the whole state. Surely Michelle would want to be best friends again. Surely my father would see me as someone special. Surely my life would be even better than it was before.

I licked my lips and held that envelope as carefully as I would hold anything valuable.

"Here goes," I said.

But I still just stood there in the science lab

surrounded by creepy things floating in jars and the smell of formaldehyde, while the Beatles Fan Club, all three of them, stared at me expectantly.

I took a breath and slipped my pointer finger in the little space between the top of the envelope and the place where the glue stops. The paper opened easily because it was white and thin so that it could fly from London, across the Atlantic Ocean, to Rhode Island and me.

"Hurry!" Nora said. "I'm about to die!"

"Maybe it's four tickets," Jessica said. Like me, she could see that the envelope was pretty full.

"That would be so cool," Peter said softly.

I pulled out the contents of the envelope and laid them on Mr. Bing's desk.

There was a letter, typed, brief, signed.

And beneath that letter, which I didn't even bother to read, was not one ticket. Or four tickets. There were, in fact, no tickets. There was just a pile of pictures of the Beatles. Publicity shots that

I'd seen in *Tiger Beat* and *Sixteen* magazines. All of them were signed, but even I knew they weren't really signed. They were stamped, fake signatures.

"'Dear Trudy Mixer,'" Jessica read, and if I wasn't so disappointed I would have grabbed my letter right out of her hands. "'Thank you for being a number one Beatles fan. Please be on the lookout for the announcement of their US tour this summer and the release of a new album!'"

Jessica handed the letter to me.

"'Sincerely, Brian Epstein,'" she said.

"The pictures are nice," Peter said.

"They're not even a little special," I said, angry. "They're dumb publicity shots."

"May I have one anyway?" Jessica asked.

I sunk into Mr. Bing's swivel desk chair. "Take them all if you want," I said.

"Really?"

"If I don't leave right now I'm going to miss the late bus, and my mother will be furious," Nora said, helping herself to a picture of George. "She likes me to cook with her when I get home," Nora added. "My mom's a great cook. She watches Julia Child."

I dropped my head in my hands. Brian Epstein hadn't even read my letter, I realized. He'd just sent me this dumb form letter and fake, signed photos. I sat like that even after they all left. My head felt like it weighed as much as the whole world weighed. In the distance I heard the Future Cheerleaders spelling out Quinn: *Give me a* Q . . . *Give me a* U . . . *Give me an* I . . . *Give me an* N . . . *Give me an* N . . . *What's that spell?*

Finally I lifted my head, and there was Peter, still sitting at a desk, looking at me.

"What do you want?" I said, not very nicely.

"I'm sorry Brian Epstein didn't send you tickets to London and a Beatles concert."

"I don't care," I mumbled. "It was just a dumb idea."

"No!" Peter said. "It was a brilliant idea."

"He didn't even read my letter. He just sent me a publicity package."

"I know, but he must be super busy—"

"Would you just leave? Please?" I said. Talking about it only made it worse.

Obviously Brian Epstein was busy. He managed *the Beatles*. But then he should get a secretary or someone to read his mail and write proper responses. My father had a secretary. Even Peterson had a secretary.

"I think you were brave to try that," Peter said at the door.

Brave? Really? Then why did I feel so stupid?

I picked up the photos that Jessica and Nora didn't take, and the dumb form letter, and that thin white airmail envelope, and threw all of it in the trash.

* * *

Even though we were having spaghetti and

meatballs, my favorite, for dinner, I was too miserable to eat.

"What was in that airmail envelope?" Mom asked. Her sweater set was a color she called coral but I called orange.

"Nothing," I said, sullen. I twirled spaghetti around my fork but just left it there.

"I thought maybe it was fan club paraphernalia," Mom said. "Do you still have that Beatles fan club?"

"Yes," I said, sounding way too defensive. "I'm only the president. That's all."

"Is something wrong with the spaghetti?" Mom asked.

I shoved a forkful into my mouth.

Dad was reading the *New York Times*, probably the Business section. His hand came around the open paper, speared a meatball, and took it back to his mouth.

"Okay," I said after I swallowed. "There was something very exciting in that envelope from

England." I said that last part really loud to get Dad's attention.

The only thing Dad and I shared these days was a mutual love of the Beatles. He was always the first one to get their new album as soon as it came out, and he'd put it on the good stereo and we'd sit side by side listening to it and studying the cover and reading bits of the liner notes to each other. It was so nice being with him like that, sometimes I wished the Beatles had a new album come out every week.

Dad didn't appear to hear me, so I said in that too-loud voice, "Yup. It was a signed letter from Brian Epstein and some very special photographs. Also signed," I added when the newspaper didn't budge.

"Isn't that nice?" Mom said. "Who exactly is Brian Epstein?"

I looked right at that newspaper and stared hard enough to bore a hole right through it into Dad's eyes.

"Only the Beatles' manager," I said.

"How in the world did you figure out how to write to him?" Mom said.

"Mom," I said, trying not to sound as exasperated as I felt, "I'm the president of the fan club! They send us all sorts of information."

Dad lowered the paper—finally!—and smiled. "Well, it was very resourceful to write directly to Brian Epstein."

I practically glowed. "Thanks," I said.

Compliments from Dad were the best because he was so smart and so busy with the big "technological boom coming our way." He was working on a big deal with some company in Japan involving semiconductors. Dad was a visionary.

"Trudy," Dad was saying. "I have a question for you. What do you think of disposable diapers?" he said.

"Um. They're a good idea?" I offered.

"Well, they would certainly free up a mother's

time. And save on water bills and electric bills," Mom said.

"That's a good point," Dad said thoughtfully.

"I don't know how Mrs. Jenkins did it," Mom said, shaking her head. "Five kids, all in diapers! Now she could have used throwaways."

I was cutting a meatball in half, then quarters, then eighths. I liked eating them symmetrically.

"Trudy," Dad said, "do you know what's happening on August eighteenth?"

"Disposable diapers?" I said.

He shook his head.

"Music in elevators?"

Dad folded the section he was reading into sharp creases so that only one piece of it was visible. Then he turned that piece toward me.

I saw a picture of the Beatles and beneath it the line: US TOUR ANNOUNCED.

"On August eighteenth," Dad said, "the Beatles are coming to Boston."

"Boston! That's practically around the corner!"

Dad laughed. "Fifty miles to be exact. And they're giving a concert at Suffolk Downs," Dad said.

He smiled at me. I smiled back. And for a tiny instant it felt like it did when we sat on the couch together listening to a new Beatles album.

CHAPTER FIVE

# Ticket to Ride

Here are things I knew:

1. Michelle's mother always dropped her off at school on Wednesday mornings because that was the day Mrs. Bee worked at her father's office. Mr. Bee was an optometrist and any kid who needed glasses, thankfully not me, went to him.

2. Because Mrs. Bee had to be at the office by 8:30, Michelle got to school early on Wednesdays, usually between 8 and 8:15.

3. No one liked to get to school early.

4. Therefore, Michelle usually hid in the library until the first bell rang at 8:30.

5. If I got to school by 7:59 and went straight to the library I would get Michelle all to myself for fifteen to thirty minutes.

6. So I got to school on Wednesday at 7:59.

* * *

Sure enough, Michelle slouched in right on schedule, at 8:10. She hadn't cut her hair like Twiggy yet, but to my surprise she had on pale pink lipstick like an eighth-grader and she smelled like lemons. Lots of lemons.

"Trudy!" she said, all awkward and surprised.

I held up *Romeo and Juliet*, which was what we were reading in English class, and recited the story I'd made up as a reason for being there.

"Yeah, I forgot my book at home yesterday so I came in early to read the homework pages." I shrugged for good measure, like *What are you gonna do?*

"Oh," Michelle said with zero interest in my story. Or me.

"You smell like lemons," I said.

"It's Love's Lemon!" she said. "Kim gave it to me."

She held her wrist out for me to sniff, which I did even though all I had to do was be in her general vicinity to catch a whiff of fake lemons.

"Nice," I said, but I felt miserable.

Michelle started looking through her purse, but I had the feeling she wasn't really looking for anything. She was just trying to seem busy to avoid talking to me.

"Did Kim give you that lipstick, too?" I asked. As soon as the words came out of my mouth, I cringed. I sounded pathetic.

"My mom let me buy it with my allowance," Michelle said, still digging around in her purse. "It's Yardley," she added.

Yardley was from London, and it's what any girl

who was allowed to wear lipstick wore because it gave you the London Look. Sometimes at the drugstore I played with the samples, swirling open the tubes and trying to decide if I'd buy Pinkadilly or Good Night Slicker or London Luv Pink when I was finally old enough.

"I got Yardley Oatmeal Soap for my birthday," I said. "Remember?"

Michelle nodded and gave me a little smile.

"Anyway," I said, "I have a huge surprise for you."

She finally stopped digging around and looked up, frowning.

"What are you doing on August eighteenth?" I asked.

"How would I know? That's, like, a million years from now."

"So you're free?" I asked.

"I don't know, Trudy," she said, and started looking through her bag again.

I decided to plunge forward.

"Well, I know what you're doing. You're coming with me and my father to Boston."

I waited, but Michelle didn't say anything.

"Do you know why we're going to Boston?" I asked her finally. "We are going to Boston to see the Beatles! In concert!"

"I don't think I can," Michelle said without looking at me.

"You don't think you can go see the Beatles? Live? Has the overly strong scent of fake lemons made you lose your mind?"

"I think I'm going to Acapulco," Michelle said.

"Mexico?"

"Kim's family goes there every summer and they stay at this hotel right on the beach."

"Michelle," I said, trying to regain my composure, "I am talking about the Beatles. In Boston."

Michelle looked me right in the eye. "The hotel is called The Princess and it's shaped like a pyramid," she said, as if that explained everything.

I stared right back at her until I saw Nora walking toward me, her hair all tangled. I could not at this crucial moment have Nora come up and talk to me. That would prove to Michelle that I was not best friend material anymore, that I was a person who someone like Nora wanted as a friend. But now Nora was grinning and waving.

"Trudy!" she said, and I realized she wasn't waving at me really. She had a newspaper clipping in her hand and that was what she was waving at me.

Michelle turned, too, and when she saw who was coming she snapped her purse shut, gathered her books, and stood up to leave.

"Did you see the Beatles' tour schedule?" Nora was saying, still waving that newspaper clipping.

"Bye, Trudy," Michelle said softly. "I don't want to interrupt your Beatles business."

"They're coming to Boston," Nora said. "The fan

club should go to the concert."

"Wait!" I called after Michelle, who had made a beeline for the door. "If the Acapulco thing falls through . . ." But she didn't hear me. She was already gone.

"If my mother lets me go," Nora was saying. "She likes to keep me close to home."

From right outside the door I heard Kim's voice. "Was that *Ger-trude* in there?"

I sighed, a big, long, sad sigh. Then I coughed, choking on Love's Lemon scent.

**\* \* \***

Every day I asked my father if the tickets had gone on sale yet and every day he said no. "Remember to get one for Michelle," I always reminded him, because what if she could come and then we didn't have a ticket for her?

"Trudy," Dad said after the millionth time I asked, "I promise you that as soon as the tickets go on sale I will buy four—three for our family and one for Michelle. So please stop pestering me."

We were at dinner, which was basically the only time I ever saw Dad and therefore the only time I could ask about the tickets and remind him about Michelle.

"Won't this be fun?" Mom said. "Maybe we can go to Durgin-Park first for dinner. What do you think, Charles?"

The *Wall Street Journal* lowered and Dad's face appeared. He didn't look very happy.

"Speaking of dinner," he said, "what is this we're eating?"

Mom beamed. "Maple Syrup Chicken," she said. "It's from *The Galloping Gourmet*."

Mom had a crush on the Galloping Gourmet, whose real name was Graham Kerr. He was English, like everything worth liking was, and he had a cooking show on in the afternoon.

Dad poked at the Maple Syrup Chicken, which was, by the way, disgusting.

"There's mushrooms in here," he said. Mom murmured yes. "And green peppers and . . . and raisins?"

"It's Indian," Mom explained. "I had to buy curry powder, which was not easy to find, believe me."

"Are these nuts?" Dad asked.

"Almonds," Mom said proudly.

Dad shook his head and returned to the *Wall Street Journal*, leaving his Maple Syrup Chicken untouched.

"How do you like it?" Mom asked me.

"It's interesting," I said, because that was the best word I could come up with.

"Yes," Mom said, smiling. "It *is* interesting."

"Dad," I said, "do you think the tickets will go on sale tomorrow?"

The *Wall Street Journal* lowered again.

"Someday very soon we are going to be required to wear safety belts when we're in the car," Dad said. "What do you two think about that?"

"Oh, Charles," Mom said, still wounded that he didn't like the Maple Syrup Chicken, "that's ridiculous."

"It's coming," Dad said. "Mark my words." He folded his newspaper into sharp neat creases and went to his study.

Mom patted my hand. "Don't worry, Trudy," she said. "He won't forget. He wants to see the Beatles almost as much as you do."

Still, I couldn't help myself. I left a note for him to find the next morning:

> *If the tickets go on sale today please please please don't forget to get one for Michelle.*

I spent a long time trying to decide how to sign it. I considered a long line of Xs and Os. I considered *Luv, Trudy*. Finally I settled on: *Luv, Your daughter Trudy* because honestly sometimes lately I wasn't so sure he remembered he had a daughter Trudy.

* * *

It seemed like a million years passed before one night Dad came home and instead of taking off his coat and hat and hanging them in the closet, then going straight to his study until dinner was ready, he walked right into the den where I was doing my New Math homework and he said, "I thought you'd be interested in this, Trudy."

"Uh-huh," I said, barely looking up because New Math was very confusing and if I paused to listen to his theory about how we were all going to have to be belted into our seats in the car then I would lose my train of thought and mess up. And if I messed up, my parents couldn't help me because this was *New* Math and they only knew how to do Old Math.

The problem I was working on was: "A logger exchanges a set L of lumber for a set M of money. The cardinality of set M is 100 and each element is worth $1." And I was doing the first part, which was to make 100 dots representing the elements of the set M. It took a very long time to make 100 dots.

"Trudy," Dad said.

"I can't. I'm counting."

"Trudy," Dad said again.

"Dad! I'm counting!"

But then I realized that Dad was actually talking to me. Or trying to. I wrote the number 76 super light near my dots and looked up.

There was Dad in his coat and hat, fanning four of the most beautiful things I'd ever seen.

"Today's the day," I said.

Dad grinned, as happy as me.

**\* \* \***

Having those tickets made almost everything seem all right. It was like they gave me special powers, and I could do anything I set my heart on doing. I got to be Juliet when the sixth grade did the balcony scene from *Romeo and Juliet* for the May Assembly. Kenny Prescott was Romeo, so

I got to stare into his eyes with those impossibly long lashes and listen to him say things like, "O, that I were a glove upon that hand, That I might touch that cheek!" to me. And I got over two dozen signatures on my petition to the vice principal to let us wear pants to school.

And then Michelle actually sat with me at lunch, even though it was only for the three days that Kim was home sick with tonsillitis. Still, we talked and laughed like we used to, and she let me try on her Yardley lipstick. She even said that if she didn't go to Acapulco she would come to the concert.

Kids came up to me in the halls and said, "How did you get those tickets?" And they called me Trudy, not *Ger-trude.*

"Oh," I said, all nonchalant, "my dad got them for me."

I started planning what to wear to the concert, even though it was still months from now. I had to look cool just in case Paul noticed me somehow.

My first-choice outfit was bell-bottoms and a peasant blouse, if I could convince my mother to buy me a pair of bell-bottoms, which in her opinion looked ridiculous. My second choice was a minidress with big squares in four different colors like one I'd seen in *Seventeen* magazine. This would only be possible if I could convince my mother to let me wear a minidress, which was unlikely. Still, I cut out the picture and stuck it on the fridge right where Mom would see it every time she had to open the refrigerator door, which was a million times a day.

The weather started to turn warm and everything looked so green—the grass and all the leaves—and sometimes I felt like I was floating instead of walking, like my feet didn't even touch the ground. On one of these perfect spring afternoons, Peter ran up to me as I was walking home from school. His glasses must have broken because there was a piece of white tape on one side, holding them together.

"My dad's trying to get tickets to the Beatles concert, too," Peter said when he caught up to me. "Maybe we can all go together?"

The last thing in the world I wanted was to have Peter and his father come with us. That would be enough to change Michelle's mind again.

"Gee, I don't think so," I said. "We're all going to Durgin-Park and stuff first so . . ."

Peter looked crushed, so I said, "If you get tickets I can check with my folks, but I'm pretty sure our plans are airtight."

"What songs do you think they'll sing?" Peter asked me after a short awkward silence passed.

"Definitely 'Yesterday,'" I said. I had been wondering this very same thing and scribbled some possible song lists in my purple notebook.

"Definitely," Peter said.

"They might play some old ones," I said. This was my wish, that the Beatles would sing "She Loves You" and "I Want to Hold Your Hand" and

"Love Me Do," all the songs that have made me their number one fan.

"Maybe," Peter said.

More awkward silence, then Peter said in a soft voice, "Do you think they'd ever record a song by a new songwriter?"

"Sure. They do it all the time. 'Anna,' and 'Chains,' and 'Twist and Shout' and—"

"No, I mean a song by someone who's not famous yet. Someone they've never even heard of."

I shrugged. "I guess. If the song's any good they might."

"But the song would have to be like the best love song ever written probably," Peter said.

Luckily, my street was the next one.

"Probably," I said, half-smiling, and turned at the corner.

"Bye, Trudy!" Peter called after me.

Once I was alone, I felt all floaty again. I could smell flowers and hear birds and the sun was just the right amount of warm.

Inside, Mom was at the stove, putting salt and pepper and onion soup mix on a pot roast.

"Oh, Trudy," she said when I walked in, and she sounded like she was not happy to see me.

I reached for a cookie from the cookie jar, fully expecting her to tell me I could have an apple or a banana but not a cookie before dinner. But she didn't say that. She just stood there with her frilly yellow apron over a lilac sweater set, looking all sad and worried. I poured a glass of milk and grabbed a second cookie before she changed her mind and forced fruit on me.

"Trudy," she said. "Dad and Peterson closed that big deal they've been working on."

"Okay," I said.

"And they are going to Japan to seal the deal with the Japanese company."

"Great," I said.

"In August," Mom said.

Just like that, my throat went dry.

"When in August?" I managed to ask.

"Dad is so disappointed—"

"You mean, we're not going to the Beatles concert?" I said.

"I'm sorry, sweetie," Mom said.

I wanted to scream. I wanted to cry. I wanted to run out of that kitchen and keep running until I couldn't run anymore. But all I could do was stand there like I was stuck to that spot, feeling the exact opposite of floaty.

# CHAPTER SIX

# Can't Buy Me Love

Things that make me angry:

1. Cream of tuna, which is Bumble Bee tuna in cream sauce with canned peas and carrots, served on toast triangles. It is exactly like cat food.

2. Speaking of cats, we can't have one. Or a dog. Because Dad is allergic. Except my mom and I suspect he isn't really allergic and uses that as an excuse to not get a cat or dog.

3. Not being able to Hula-Hoop without

dropping it for as long as Theresa Mazzoni.

4. Most days, Theresa Mazzoni.

5. How President Johnson won't end the Vietnam War. (He makes me feel very conflicted because I adore his wife, Lady Bird Johnson. She started the Make America Beautiful campaign and got rid of litter on the highways and planted flowers on the median strips. Why is someone like her married to Lyndon Johnson?)

6. The *Wall Street Journal*. The *New York Times*. And every other newspaper that my father hides behind at dinner every night.

7. Pop quizzes.

8. Frank Sinatra songs. In particular the album *Sinatra's Sinatra*, which Mom plays all the time. I swear, if I have to hear "Call Me Irresponsible" one more time I will run screaming from the

house. Also: "I've Got You Under My Skin," "In the Wee Small Hours of the Morning," and "Nancy."

9. Mom singing "Nancy," loud, while she vacuums. *Keep Betty Grable, Lamour, and Turner, She makes my heart a charcoal burner, It's heaven when I embrace, My Nancy with the laughin' face!* "Stop, stop, please," I beg her. But she just keeps vacuuming and keeps singing that dumb song. Betty Grable, Dorothy Lamour, and Lana Turner are movie stars from a million years ago, that's how old-fashioned that song is. Sometimes I follow behind her and sing "Eight Days a Week" at the top of my lungs. But between the noise of the vacuum and her own singing, she doesn't even care.

10. When someone calls me Gertrude. As soon as I'm eighteen I'm going to court

to legally change my name to Trudy. Or maybe to Ariel. Or Ariadne. Anything but Gertrude.

11. Future Cheerleaders.

12. Lately, Michelle.

13. Japan.

# CHAPTER SEVEN

# Baby, You Can Drive My Car

The next morning I woke up with a plan. An obvious plan. Mom would just have to take me to the Beatles concert. There was one obstacle to this plan however: Mom did not like to drive. At all. Whenever we go on a family vacation, like the time we went to Niagara Falls or last Columbus Day weekend, when we went leaf peeping in Vermont, Dad does all the driving because Mom doesn't like highways, winding roads, traffic, parallel parking, or driving when it's dark. Mostly, she just drives to the grocery store or the bank, little local trips like that. And even then, if her sister—my aunt

Florence—offers to take her, Mom always says yes.

So although I had an obvious plan, convincing Mom that she needed to take me to the concert was going to be hard. Especially because Boston was notorious for having the worst, most aggressive drivers in the entire country. Dad had read that in the *New York Times*.

Still, I arrived at the breakfast table ready to launch my campaign. Dad was already gone and Mom was already sitting at the little table in the kitchen where we ate breakfast and lunch, looking at her seed catalogs. We called that area The Nook because it was set back from the rest of the kitchen in a small alcove with a big window that looked out at our backyard. My swing set was still back there, even though I couldn't remember the last time I'd used it. The birdbath Dad gave Mom for her birthday was there, too, and the small garden where Mom grew tomatoes and green peppers and mint. I liked sitting in The Nook.

It was bright and sunny and we ate off colorful melamine dishes instead of the fancier ones we used in the dining room. *Melamine* is just a big word for plastic, but Mom says it sounds better.

"Good morning," I chirped, and Mom looked up with a big smile.

"I knew you'd feel better in the morning," she said. She poured me some orange juice, dropped two pieces of French toast on an orange melamine plate, and slid the Mrs. Butterworth's syrup over to me.

Since I had only picked at my dinner last night, I was starving, and dug right in.

"The Beatles will have another concert next year," Mom said, "and we will definitely go to it."

"What if this is their last concert ever?" I said.

"Don't be ridiculous, Trudy. Why would this be their last concert?"

"Michelle says they might break up."

"The Beatles?" Mom said, chuckling. "Honey, I

can assure you that the Beatles are never going to break up. They're the most popular group in the world."

"But what if they did? And we missed our only chance to see them in person?"

"That's not going to happen, Trudy. Don't be so dramatic."

I concentrated on my French toast while Mom poured herself another cup of coffee.

When she sat down again I came right out with it. "Mom, I think you should take Michelle and me to the concert."

"Me?" she said. "How in the world would I do that?"

"You could drive us," I said.

"To Boston?" Mom said, and she actually put one hand to her chest, like she was having a heart attack just thinking about driving to Boston. "Oh no."

"I was thinking we could do practice runs. You

and me. Like on Saturdays. You could drive a little bit more each week, and by the time August comes you'll be prepared."

"Trudy, Boston has the worst, most—"

"—aggressive drivers. I know."

I put on my martyr face, the one I wore when I went to the dentist or when Mom asked me to go shopping with her instead of to Michelle's house on a Saturday afternoon.

"Don't look like that," Mom said.

"Like what?" I said, all innocent.

"Like that!" Mom said.

I kept looking like that.

"Fine," Mom said finally. "I will try these practice runs, but if I get nervous or people honk at me, I'm stopping."

I stopped my martyr face so that I could get up and hug Mom.

"You can do it," I whispered into her Arpège-smelling neck. "You're the best."

\* \* \*

The first Saturday, we didn't get very far. Mom was driving like thirty miles an hour on Route 95 and everybody passed her, which made her nervous.

"Too many cars whizzing past," she said, and got off the highway and drove home.

But after three weeks, we made it all the way to Providence, a distance of thirteen and a half miles. To celebrate, we went shopping for spring coats at Gladding's department store and had Salisbury steaks at Alexander's for lunch. At this rate, I thought, it would take Mom all the way until August to drive the sixty-three and a half miles to Boston.

"Wasn't this fun?" Mom said as we drove back home. She still drove way too slow on Route 95, and cars still passed her. It just seemed to bother her less.

"I knew you could do it, Mom," I said.

And she did. By June, she drove right to Suffolk

Downs, where the concert was going to be. She was nervous, but also proud.

"Here we are, Trudy," she said, pointing to it.

Suffolk Downs was actually a horse racetrack, but that was the kind of place the Beatles played—Shea Stadium in New York, Crosley Field in Cincinnati, Candlestick Park in San Francisco. That way thousands of their fans could see their concerts. Like me.

I stared at that building and tried to imagine being inside, watching the Beatles take the stage, hearing them sing "I Saw Her Standing There," and seeing with my own eyes how they shake their heads after they sing *I'll never dance with another, since I saw her standing there* and their mop tops fly around like they did on *The Ed Sullivan Show*. Peter and I still debate what songs they'll sing, but I really believe that somehow they will sing all of my favorite ones, like they're singing just to me.

**\* \* \***

In the Beatles Fan Club we worked on making a big sign for me to bring to the concert. Nora thought it should just say WE LOVE YOU! Jessica thought if the sign only said that then we should spell LOVE like LUV. Peter thought it should rhyme, and I thought my name should be on it. It only took forever for us to agree on what the sign would say. Finally we settled on THE ROBERT E. QUINN BEATLES FAN CLUB LOVES THE BEATLES!!! Which was way too many words, so we had to kind of squish them together. Nora wanted us to use bubble letters, but bubble letters are way too fat, and even with squishing the words, they wouldn't fit. Jessica was the best at art, so we let her write it, and I insisted on blue because that was Paul's favorite color. Nora thought we should alternate blue with red (Ringo's favorite color), purple (George's), and green (John's). But I was the president after all, so I vetoed that idea.

"I wish I was going to the concert," Jessica said.

"Me too," Nora said. "But my mom would never let me. She likes me to stay home with her."

Nora's mom sounded a little weird to me, always wanting Nora home with her instead of doing normal twelve-year-old things.

I put on *The Beatles' Second Album*, and Peter sighed.

"This is my favorite album," he said.

Just then, Michelle walked by in her dumb cheerleader's uniform, which was a short red pleated skirt, and inside the pleats was white, and a white sweater with a red *Q* on it, and white ankle socks and sneakers.

"Michelle!" I called to her.

She hesitated. "I've got practice," she said.

"Sure," I said. "Just come look at our sign."

"To take to the concert," Peter said.

Michelle stepped inside, though just over the threshold, not all the way in. For an instant, it was like it used to be, the Beatles singing in the background and Michelle here. I thought about how many kids used to be in the fan club, the room hot and crowded because there were so many of us, and how sometimes I put on "Twist and Shout" and everybody practiced doing the twist.

Jessica and Nora held up the sign—it took two people because it was so big.

"Nice," Michelle said, sounding very polite.

"Do you think Paul will see it from the stage when we hold it up?" I asked her.

Michelle blinked a bunch of times.

"Actually," she said, "I'm going to Acapulco. With Kim. I thought I told you."

Just then, the record came to the end so the room went completely silent. I wished someone would flip it over, just so there'd be noise. But no one did.

"Well, you said you might not go," I said into the quiet. "So I thought . . ."

"Oh, well, I'm going now," she said again.

She started to leave but paused first. "I hope Paul sees it," she said. "I hope Paul sees you, Trudy." And then off she went.

Jessica and Nora were still holding the sign and the needle of the record player kept skipping along the empty groove.

"I can go in her place," Peter said hopefully.

I tried to decide what would be worse: going to the concert with just my mother, or going with my mother and the nerdiest boy in sixth grade. Definitely the latter.

Even though I kept telling myself that it didn't matter that Michelle wasn't coming and therefore I was going to a concert with my mother, it still mattered. Every time I felt bad about it, I reminded myself that I was going to see the Beatles—the Beatles! But deep down I knew that I really liked having a best friend, and I didn't have one anymore.

In fact, I didn't have any friends now. In the halls at school, some kids were still calling me

*Ger-trude.* I was still stuck having to eat lunch with Jessica. She'd started collecting good-luck charms—a metal four-leaf clover, a gross rabbit's foot, a penny from the year she was born. Every time she got a new one, she showed it to me and explained why it was good luck.

"You know," she told me, "not every rabbit's foot is good luck. It has to be the left hind foot. And the rabbit has to be caught in a cemetery. During a full moon."

She was stroking that creepy thing right near my American chop suey.

"Some people believe the rabbit has to be shot with a silver bullet. But some people say the foot has to be cut off while the rabbit's still alive."

"Ugh," I said, pushing my tray away.

"Do you think that matters?" Jessica asked me, all serious.

When she got that cheap metal four-leaf clover it was the same thing. "Four-leaf clovers are lucky because they're so rare," she told me.

I looked at hers. The green paint was already chipping off. "I think that only pertains to *real* four-leaf clovers," I said.

"The first leaf is for faith," Jessica continued, as if I hadn't said anything. "The second is for hope. The third is for love. And the fourth is for luck."

Across the cafeteria the gaggle of Future Cheerleaders broke into loud giggles. I strained my neck to try to see what was so funny.

"I wish I could find a real one," Jessica said sadly. "Then I'd have good luck for sure."

Kenny Prescott walked past our table and under his breath he said, *"Ger-trude,"* as if he hadn't just been my Romeo.

I put my face in my hands and told myself that I was the only kid in the whole school that was going to see the Beatles. But I didn't feel any better.

**\* \* \***

Then, just when I thought things couldn't get

worse, they did. Dad calls this Murphy's Law: Anything that can go wrong, will go wrong.

I came home from school after another miserable day. At lunch Jessica told me a ladybug had landed on her knee. "That's supposed to be good luck," she said, "right?" I actually told her I had forgotten to do something for homework and went to sit with Peter and two other nerdy boys. They were debating if it was possible to swallow a tablespoon of cinnamon.

"I'm telling you, it blocks your saliva glands," Richard Harriman said through his mouthful of braces.

"Seriously," Leo Spitz said, "don't even try. It can kill you."

I chewed my dry hamburger. By the time I made it through the lunch line, they had run out of ketchup.

That afternoon, I wanted nothing more than to get home and watch TV, even my mother's boring soap opera *Another World.*

Except when I got home, my mother wasn't there. The house was empty and silent.

Still, I called out, "Mom?" as if she might pop out of a closet or something.

In the kitchen, *The Fannie Farmer Cookbook* was opened to a recipe for Stuffed Pork Chops, and there were four pork chops sitting on butcher's paper on the counter beside some chopped-up apples.

Before I could get too worried, the door flew open and our neighbor Mrs. Bellow ran in. Dad said it was appropriate her last name was Bellow because that's exactly what she did when she talked.

"Oh, you're home!" she said in her too-loud voice. "Now don't panic but your mother was taken away in an ambulance."

"What?" I said. Maybe I even bellowed.

"She's fine, she's fine—"

"People who are fine don't get taken away in ambulances," I said.

"Well, not fine exactly. But nothing serious. She just broke her leg."

"What?" I said again, definitely bellowing.

"I saw it with my own eyes," Mrs. Bellow said. "She went outside to get the mail and tripped and fell down the front steps. I called the ambulance and stayed with her until your father showed up at the emergency room. Just a cast for twelve weeks. No swimming or standing or driving."

"No driving?"

"Bones heal!" Mrs. Bellow said.

I thought about poor Mom in a big cast for the whole hot summer. But I thought about me, too. And the Beatles concert she was supposed to drive me to in just eight short weeks. Murphy's Law: Anything that can go wrong, will go wrong.

# CHAPTER EIGHT

# Girl

It is not fun being around someone with a broken leg. First of all, that person—aka Mom—is miserable. Broken legs hurt. A lot. And the cast weighs about a million pounds. Also, it's impossible to get around. Even small trips, like from the sofa to the kitchen for a glass of water, take so much time and energy that Mom decided it wasn't worth it. "Let me die of thirst," she groaned. In other words, I couldn't be mad at Mom for not being able to drive me to the Beatles concert. But I could be mad at the mail, which is what she was on her way to pick up when she fell. And the front step that had a weird little buckle in it, probably from the winter cold. "Frost heaves," Dad said, shaking his head and examining what had caused Mom to trip. I could be mad at the universe or whatever was responsible for the bad luck I'd had ever since Mrs. Peabody changed me from Trudy to Gertrude. And I was mad at all those things.

The next day in school, as I made my sorry way to second period, social studies with Mrs. Peabody, an eighth-grade girl who I knew to be Penelope Mayer came up to me in the hall. She had the longest, straightest, auburnest hair in maybe the entire world and just the right sprinkling of freckles across her cheeks and nose. Why is someone called Penelope and not the cuter nickname Penny considered cool, and another person—me, for example—who is suddenly Gertrude rather than Trudy, a social pariah? I didn't know the answer. But now that the lovely Penelope was walking by my side, and smiling her smile that was so bright stars practically shone off her teeth, all I could do was accept my own fate and bask in Penelope's presence.

"You're Gertrude Mixer, right?" Penelope said.

I cringed. "Trudy," I said through clenched teeth.

Penelope tossed her hair. Or maybe she just moved her head and the tossing was a kind of by-product of any movement.

"I heard you're going to see the Beatles? In Boston?"

Up close I saw that Penelope's eyes were as enchanting as the rest of her—a soft brown that brought to mind Hershey's kisses.

"Uh," I said, the way people who are under a spell or hypnotized do. "You smell good," I blurted, stupidly.

Penelope smiled. Imagine bright stars. "Patchouli," she said.

I nodded, also stupidly.

She motioned with her chin to the room across from Mrs. Peabody's. "This is me," she said. "Spanish."

"Adios," I said, which was one of the very few words I knew in Spanish.

Penelope laughed. "You're funny," she said. "It's so cool that you're going to the concert. I am, too. With a boy," she added. "He's in high school."

"Wow," I said, impressed. *High school?*

I watched her disappear, swallowed up in a group of other cool girls. They certainly weren't in Future Cheerleaders, I thought with great satisfaction. In fact, Penelope was the president of the Poets Club.

The second bell rang, jolting me out of my Penelope stupor. I scurried to class, but not before I caught Michelle and Kim staring in disbelief at me. They'd seen me with Penelope.

"She's going to the Beatles concert, too," I said as I passed them.

*Take that*, I thought, almost happily.

But of course, I *wasn't* going to the concert. Mom had a broken leg and it was going to stay broken until August. All I had were four tickets and a big sign.

\* \* \*

The last day of school finally arrived. It was such a relief to have the worst school year of my life come to an end. My brief encounter with greatness, also known as Penelope Mayer, was soon forgotten by everyone who'd witnessed it. In no time, I was back to *Ger-trude*, president of the after-school club with the fewest members. I had tickets to a Beatles concert in my possession, but no one to go with and no way to get there. Summer loomed, as bleak as the rest of the year had been.

On the Saturday after the last day of school, Dad announced that I had to go to the mall and get Mom all the things on a very long list she'd written on the little pad where she wrote all of her lists. At the top of the paper there was a picture of a melon and the words *Honey Do!* Nora said that things like that were sexist, that women shouldn't expect men to do things for them. I guess she was right, but Dad and I like puns, so it didn't bother me.

Anyway, Dad would wait in the car while I completed the Honey Do list; he hated the mall, and shopping in general.

"Dad, I can't go to the mall alone. That is socially unacceptable," I explained.

"Trudy," Dad said, "we need to help Mom in every way we can."

I looked at Mom's list.

· Women's housedresses, size medium,
various colors and patterns. Not too loud.
· Knitting needles, extra long
· A small but loud bell
· Magazines: Good Housekeeping, Ladies'
Home Journal, Redbook, Gourmet

"What if someone sees me buying this stuff?" I shrieked. "Knitting needles?"

"I need them to scratch inside my cast, Trudy," Mom called from her perch on the sofa.

*"Ladies' Home Journal*?"

"I'm bored, Trudy," Mom grumbled. "You try sitting for a month."

Dad, who had been reading graphs and diagrams, stood.

"Let's go so we can get back," he said, which was typical Dad logic.

Of course I had to do it. Mom hobbled to the kitchen on her crutches exactly three times a day, muttering and wincing, to make us food. Otherwise, she just sat there with her leg in that enormous cast. Plus, it was impossible to explain to Dad that going to the mall alone—never mind buying knitting needles in the Notions Department at Woolworth's—was almost as bad as sitting with Jessica in her Girl Scout uniform at lunch.

ANN HOOD

"Don't dillydally in there," Dad said when he dropped me off at the entrance to the mall.

As if I wanted to prolong my solitary excursion in the Mrs. Department of Jordan Marsh.

"That won't be a problem," I said.

*　*　*

The mall was crowded with kids from all over the state. School was out. It wasn't warm enough yet to go to the beach. And *The Russians Are Coming, The Russians Are Coming* was playing. A perfect Saturday was to walk around the mall, touch everything at Spencer Gifts, pretend to look at books at Waldenbooks but really look at the cute boy who worked there, pretend to look at records but really look at the cute boy who worked at RecordLand, eat cheeseburgers at Newport Creamery, and go to the movies. And that was exactly what the entire population of kids was doing—having a perfect Saturday. With one exception: me.

I kept my head down and moved through

Jordan Marsh fast. First, the housedresses, those ugly loose-fitting cotton dresses that Mom sometimes refers to as muumuus because it sounds exotic, Hawaiian even, while *housedresses* sounds matronly and the exact opposite of exotic. I yanked four off the rack without really looking at them too closely, and got the heck out of the Mrs. Department as fast as I could. I recognized some girls from school when I zipped past the Junior Department. They were holding teeny bikinis up to their bodies and asking each other for opinions. I kept walking.

Woolworth's was practically empty except for some old ladies buying plastic flowers and young mothers with screaming babies buying baby stuff. Of course as soon as I walked in, a parakeet escaped from the Pet Department, because that happened every five minutes at Woolworth's. The bird dive-bombed the old ladies. Someone screamed. A stock boy rushed past with a butterfly net. Luckily, I saw no one that I knew. I found Notions, chose the longest knitting needles they had, and got out of there. The parakeet was still not caught when I left.

Waldenbooks would be a lot trickier, since everybody went in there to gaze at the cute guy. He had too-long hair that fell into his eyes and over his collar and he wore a bored expression like he didn't notice all the girls hovering around him. His name tag said MARC. With a C! This only added to his allure.

Head down, I slithered into the bookstore. I saw lots of flip-flopped feet with pale pink toenails standing by the paperback best sellers, which were right near the cash register, which was where Marc presided. I headed to Magazines, on the opposite wall. Basically, Mom just wanted women's magazines, the kind that offered recipes, makeup tips, clothing trends, gardening advice, and articles about how to stay married or overcome horrible luck. She'd made a list, but I just plucked anything that had an actress on the cover and the word *recipes* in big letters.

Then I heard the worst thing I could have heard.

"Gertrude?"

Slowly, I lifted my head. And looked straight into the soft brown eyes of Penelope.

"Hi!" she said.

She had on bell-bottoms and a gauzy flowered shirt and a droopy straw hat. And she was holding a magazine I'd never heard of before. *The New Yorker.*

"They run poems every week," she explained. "And two short stories. And cartoons that I don't really understand most of the time."

I tried to think of something smart to say, but there I was with a bag full of housedresses, two giant knitting needles, and an armful of magazines.

"Did you hear the Beatles have a new album coming out?" Penelope asked me.

"Yeah," I said. "In August!"

"Right before the concert!"

"Right," I said, and my stomach felt like I'd just swallowed stones.

"I can't wait," Penelope said. "It's going to be the highlight of the whole summer. Maybe of the whole year."

Looking at Penelope, a thought struck me.

"Hey," I said, trying to think of the best way to ask what I wanted to ask. "Is that high-school boy . . . um . . . sixteen?"

She beamed. "He will be. In July," she said. She lowered her voice. "My parents would kill me if they knew."

"So . . . you guys are . . . driving to the concert, I guess."

There. I'd said it. Now I just had to get up the courage to ask her if I could get a ride with them.

"Oh no," Penelope said, wrinkling her nose. "We're taking the bus. The Bonanza? From Providence?"

SHE LOVES YOU (YEAH, YEAH, YEAH)

"The Bonanza," I said, those stones suddenly gone.

"One hour!" Penelope said. She lowered her voice. "We did it before, to see the Young Rascals. In April. And we made out the whole way there and back."

"Wow," I said.

Penelope giggled. "It's so much fun," she said.

"Wow," I said again, not sure if she meant taking the bus or making out. I had never met anyone who had made out with a boy.

"See you around, Gertrude," Penelope said, sliding the magazine back on the rack. "I hope!"

When she walked away, she tinkled. Around her ankles was a delicate silver chain with tiny silver bells.

Bells!

The last thing on my list.

By the time I got back into the car, my father

waiting impatiently, I felt like a new person. There was a bus to Boston. And on August 18, I was going to be on it.

"Finally," Dad said. He practically had the car in gear before I even closed my door.

"There was a parakeet loose in Woolworth's," I told him.

His mouth was moving silently, the way it did when he was thinking his own thoughts.

I frowned. "Dad," I said, "a parakeet was flying all around Woolworth's and some poor stock boy was chasing it with a butterfly net."

He grunted. Sort of.

"Then it landed on a lady's head and she started to scream and go kind of crazy. Turns out she has an irrational fear of birds."

I waited. Nothing.

"Maybe from that Hitchcock movie?" I tried.

More nothing.

"Anyway, they took her away in a straitjacket."

"What, Trudy?" Dad said vaguely. "This is not true, is it?"

I sighed an exasperated sigh.

"The Beatles have a new album coming out on August eighth," I said, now that I had a little bit of his attention.

"They do? We have to be first in line to get it," he said.

I could picture it, me and Dad waiting at Record-Land, buying the album, marveling over its cover design, holding our breath until we could get it home and put it on the stereo. We'd sit side by side, listening in bliss. And for maybe forty-five whole minutes, I would have Dad to myself.

"Here's what we'll do," Dad was saying. "Get up early. Go to Dunkin' Donuts. Get to the mall an hour before it opens so we'll be first in line. Those doors open and we make a beeline for Record-Land so we can see what our Mr. McCartney has done this time."

This time it was me who was only half-listening. An idea was taking hold in me. A very good idea. And if I could make it happen, then Dad would surely know that he had the most amazing, wonderful, smartest, fabulous kid ever.

# CHAPTER NINE

# Day Tripper

One very good thing about having an immobile mother was that I could do practically anything I wanted. I was mostly out of view. Even though all day I was at her beck and call—*Trudy, bring some iced tea please! Trudy, change the channel please? Trudy, turn on the fan!*—I was pretty much free to roam around the house, as long as I was in earshot. What with broken legs and trips to Japan, everybody seemed to forget about those four Beatles tickets on my parents' dresser. Everyone except me. One day I slipped them into my hands and hid them in my sock drawer and no one even noticed.

Every other summer I went to day camp at the playground down the street. We sat in the shade and did crafts, like macramé plant holders, gimp bracelets, and gluing shells onto small boxes. Sometimes the counselors, who were only a few years older than us, organized games of kickball or tag, but they mostly just liked to huddle together and talk about boys they liked. If we were lucky, they turned on the sprinkler after lunch and we got to run through it. It was the most boring thing ever, so when Mom announced that I had to miss camp to help her out this summer, I was delighted.

Now that I had a plan to set into motion, I was even happier. I had all day to work on it.

First, I had to figure out how to get that bus to Boston.

I pulled the phone cord as far as it could stretch so that I was away from Mom, and grabbed the Yellow Pages from the cupboard where we kept them and the White Pages and Mom's personal telephone numbers. I loved looking things up in the Yellow Pages, like businesses that sold reptiles and businesses that built sheds. Who knew there were so many weird businesses out there, nestled between plumbing companies and dentists and shoe stores. I loved the White Pages, too. So many people lived in Rhode Island! Once, I found shelves of White Pages from all around the country in the library basement. New York City had its own White Pages because so many people lived there. California needed two volumes, but Wyoming's was skinny, skinnier than Rhode Island's. That day I looked up Gertrude Mixer in as many states as I could. But there wasn't even one other Gertrude Mixer anywhere, which made me feel special, even though I had the worst name ever.

When I told Mom that I was the only Gertrude Mixer in the United States, she told me that women never listed their names in the White Pages. So Gertrude Mixer would be listed as G.

Mixer. That way strangers wouldn't have her phone number. "Well," I told Mom, "when I have my own apartment and my phone number is listed in the White Pages, my name will be T. Mixer, not G. Mixer."

Anyway, today I needed to look up Bus Lines, so it was the fat Yellow Pages that I heaved out of the cupboard. I flipped to *B*, and there it was, just like Penelope told me: BONANZA BUS LINES. The ad beside the phone number said: DAILY SERVICE BETWEEN PROVIDENCE BOSTON LOGAN AIRPORT CAPE COD. I carefully dialed the number listed and counted seven rings before a woman answered.

"Bonanza Bus Lines, how may I help you?"

I lowered my voice so I sounded older. "What time do your buses go to Boston from Providence?"

"Every hour on the hour, returning every hour on the half," she said. She must have answered this question a lot because she sounded kind of like a robot.

"Can the bus drop me off at Suffolk Downs?" I asked her.

She hesitated. "Well, no. It drops you off at the bus terminal." She didn't sound so mechanical anymore.

"Do you know how far that is from Suffolk Downs?"

"No, but I'm sure you can get a taxi at the terminal."

I had Mom's little Honey Do notepad and a pen so I could write everything down, and so far, even though I just had when the buses ran, bus terminal, and taxi written down, this plan was getting kind of complicated.

"Okay," I said, trying to think.

"Is there anything else I can help you with?" she said, back to her robot voice.

"No. Wait. Yes. How much is a ticket?"

"One way or round-trip?"

"Round-trip."

"Five dollars and fifty cents," she said.

I wrote that down, too.

After I hung up, I stared at my list. There were some obstacles already and I hadn't even started working out the details of my new, bigger plan.

* * *

Mom was especially needy that day. I spent most of my time running around adjusting the fan and the pillows under her leg, turning the TV on and off or changing the channels, fetching her drinks and snacks, lifting and lowering the shades. It was hot and humid and her leg was itchy and smelly. But all the mindless activity gave me time to figure out what to do. Getting to the concert was not as easy as I'd thought before I talked to the Bonanza Bus lady. I made a mental list of problems: getting to the bus station in Providence, getting to Suffolk Downs from the bus terminal in Boston, and getting back to the terminal after the concert. Penelope had made it sound so easy!

Penelope, I realized as soon as I had that thought. I would ask her how to get from here to there and there to here. As soon as I brought Mom a bowl of blueberries and readjusted her pillows, I looked up Penelope's phone number and called her. This was, of course, terrifying. Someone like me—*Ger-trude!*—did not call one of the coolest kids in school. But she'd been so friendly to me. And we were both going to the Beatles concert, so we had the most important thing in common. Of course I didn't expect Penelope to be home. She was probably at the beach or the mall or making out somewhere with that high-school boy.

To my utter surprise, Penelope herself answered the phone. She sounded 100 percent bored until I said it was me, Trudy ... um ... Gertrude ... Mixer.

"Hi!" she said. "Wow! This is great!"

*It is?* I thought. But what I said was that I'd called to talk about the concert.

"As it turns out," I said, "I'm taking the bus, too."

"You are? Cool!" Penelope said.

I laid out my problems and Penelope said, "Oh, it's easy. You catch a bus on Providence Street to downtown. And when you get to the bus terminal in Boston, you take the T to Suffolk Downs."

"The T," I repeated.

"Right. The subway," Penelope said, and she didn't sound at all like she thought I was dumb or anything.

"Ah," I said.

"It's super easy," Penelope said.

"Sure," I said.

"It helps when you're with other people, so they can double-check that you're going in the right direction and stuff."

"Sure," I said again.

"I never asked," Penelope said. "Who are you going with?"

"The Beatles Fan Club," I said without even thinking.

"Oh! Of course! If I wasn't running the Poets Club, I would be in the fan club."

"You would?" I said.

Penelope laughed softly. "Thanks for calling."

"Bye," I said, realizing I should have been thanking her, not the other way around.

"Hey!" Penelope said. "Look for me at the concert? I'm in row M, seat twenty-one."

Then there was the click of her hanging up.

Mom was calling, "Trudy! Come turn off this television before I lose my mind!"

"Coming!" I said.

But I wasn't coming. I was adding to my Honey Do list. Why hadn't I thought of it before? Even though they were the least cool kids in the school and I didn't want to be seen with any of them, the three remaining members of the Beatles Fan Club had to come to the concert with me. They were the only other people who cared as much as I did about getting there. And when they heard what else I had planned, they wouldn't be able to refuse.

\* \* \*

If I had called Michelle or Kim or even Hannah Mazzy, who was popular in a bad way—for example, she liked the Rolling Stones and her brother had actually been in jail—and asked them if they could come to my house the next afternoon, the answer would be no. Not just because they had no interest in coming to my house but also because they were busy. Busy going to the beach or sitting in front of a fan in someone's bedroom listening to records or, in Hannah's case, busy playing Frisbee at Goddard Park. Other kids were busy at camp—day camp or even sleepaway camp in New Hampshire or someplace.

But all three members of the Robert E. Quinn Beatles Fan Club were absolutely, 100 percent available. Jessica did go to Girl Scout camp, but not until the end of July. And Peter went to visit his father's relatives in Indiana, but also not until the end of July. Mostly, they did nothing all summer.

For the emergency meeting I made fudgies, which were basically oats, melted chocolate, and peanut butter shaped into cookies, dropped on wax paper, and put in the fridge for a couple of hours, and a pitcher of cherry Kool-Aid. I asked Mom to please not need anything between one and three, left her the pile of magazines and snacks, and closed the living room door to dull the sound of the television. I put on *Meet the Beatles*, a nostalgic choice, being that it was the Beatles' very first album, and I hoped that would help my case. After all, I was going to ask the fan club to lie, steal, and run away. I needed all the help I could get.

At 12:45, exactly fifteen minutes early, I heard Nora outside calling *Goodbye, Mom! Thanks for the lift! Love you, too!*

I rolled my eyes, not just at how dorky Nora was but also at the fact that she arrived fifteen whole minutes early. Hadn't she ever heard of being fashionably late? Luckily, I was ready. The pitcher of Kool-Aid was nice and cold and the fudgies were on Mom's good platter, the one decorated with daisies.

When the doorbell rang and I went to open the door, not only was Nora standing there but so was Jessica, in her Girl Scout uniform. Maybe it was my imagination but the merit badges on her sash seemed to have tripled.

She must have seen me looking because she grinned and touched her sash and said, "I decided to get a badge a week this summer. It's my goal."

Before they even walked inside Peter came riding up on his bicycle. I only hoped Theresa, my next-door neighbor who went to Catholic school, didn't see him because having a boy like Peter ride his bike to your house was about the most embarrassing thing I could imagine. Theresa was a year older and rolled up the waistband of her kelly green and navy blue plaid skirt as soon as she rounded the corner out of sight. She also unbuttoned her white blouse one extra button. Which is to say she was not a girl you wanted to see someone like Peter, on his bike.

I hurried the three of them in and led them to the kitchen. It was only 12:50.

After they all took glasses of Kool-Aid and cookies I announced that I was calling the first ever summer emergency fan club meeting to order.

They waited, expectantly. I couldn't help but notice that Peter's nose and cheeks were sunburned and Nora's bangs were cut kind of crooked, like maybe she'd cut them herself.

Very dramatically, and slowly, I pulled the four Beatles concert tickets from my pocket.

"As you can see, these are tickets to the Beatles concert in Boston on August eighteenth," I said, fanning the tickets on the table.

"Wow," Peter said in a soft voice.

"Can I, like, touch them?" Nora said.

I let her hold them for a few seconds.

"Due to circumstances out of my control that involve international travel and medical emergencies, three of these tickets have become available," I said.

They just stared at me, still waiting.

"And it seems only appropriate that they should go to the Beatles Fan Club," I said.

Now it was my turn to wait. But nobody said anything.

"I mean," I said finally, "you guys."

"My mom won't let me go," Nora said. "No way."

"I have camp," Jessica said.

"I am the luckiest person alive," Peter said.

I took a deep breath.

"Jessica," I said evenly, "this is the chance of a lifetime. There are rumors that the Beatles might break up—"

"What?" Nora gasped.

"—and this could be your only chance in your entire life to see them in concert," I finished.

"Well," Nora said, staring at the fake straw place mats I'd set out, "maybe I can convince her."

I turned to Jessica. "I thought you had camp in July."

"I do. But if I earn more than a dozen merit badges by August fifteenth, I get a free week. It's a really huge honor," Jessica added.

"Is it huger than seeing the Beatles?" I asked her. "Seriously?"

"It's just that I'm working really hard on badges like Archery and Botany and Reading. I mean, I have to read ten books for that badge, plus all the other stuff."

Frankly, Jessica looked pretty miserable. She was working herself to death, and it was only the first week of July.

"Jessica," I said, "we are talking about the Beatles."

"The *Beatles*!" Peter said.

I appreciated his enthusiasm.

"I don't know," Jessica said. "I made this goal and I want to reach it."

"How are we going to get there?" Peter said, ready to plan.

But without Jessica and Nora on board, how could I tell them what I needed to tell them? Unless my new plan was so spectacular—which it was—that it would convince them.

"So we need to take the bus to Boston—"

Nora looked terrified. "The bus?" she said.

"It's super easy," I said. "I've done it like a million times. You just get on the bus to Providence from right in front of the fire station and then at the station in Providence you connect to Bonanza."

"Does the fan club have any money left over from the Beatlemania sale?" Jessica asked.

"Unfortunately no," I admitted.

Last spring we'd had a big sale one Saturday where people could sell or trade Beatles records and memorabilia. But we'd used all eighteen dollars on stamps and envelopes for fan letters, stuff to make signs, and a fan club copy of *Rubber Soul* when it came out.

"But bus tickets are only six dollars. Round-trip," I added for emphasis.

"I don't have six dollars," Nora said.

"Can't you ask your mom?" I said.

"No," Nora said quickly.

"I have four dollars already," Peter said hopefully.

Jessica's eyes lit up. "We can have a lemonade stand and that will help me get my Entrepreneur badge."

I wondered if this meant she was coming, but before I could confirm that, she frowned.

"Of course I wasn't going to work on that badge—"

"But now you are!" Peter said. "And we're going to help you, so it will be really easy."

"I guess," Jessica said, obviously thinking.

"Okay," I said, "then we'll take the subway to Suffolk Downs, which is also super easy."

Now Nora was looking worried.

"Then we'll see the concert and then we will do the most important fan club business we've ever *ever* done," I said.

Nora looked even more worried.

"After the concert, we are going straight to the Parker House Hotel. Do you know why?"

Jessica shook her head.

"Because we are going to meet Paul McCartney. And get his autograph. And show up at school in September as the only kids in the entire school who actually met Paul McCartney," I said.

"We can actually talk to him?" Peter said, his eyes shiny with excitement and big dreams.

"Yes," I said, as if I knew this as a fact.

"How are we ever going to meet Paul McCartney?" Nora said.

"That's what this emergency meeting is all about," I said. "We have to figure that out."

# CHAPTER TEN

# Help!

OPERATION MEET PAUL MCCARTNEY

THE ROBERT E. QUINN BEATLES FAN CLUB

PLAN A:

*August 18, 1966*

1. Jessica and Trudy tell parents they
   are having a sleepover at Nora's. Nora
   tells parents she is sleeping over at
   Trudy's. Peter tells parents he is on a
   campout with sixth-grade boys for team
   building.

2. Meet at the RIPTA bus stop in front of

fire station on Providence Street at
1 p.m.

3. Board 1:15 bus to Providence.
(IMPORTANT: ACT LIKE YOU DO THIS
EVERY DAY!!!)

4. Arrive at bus terminal at 2 p.m. Buy
tickets for bus to Boston.

5. Board 3 p.m. bus to Boston,
arrive 4 p.m. (IMPORTANT: LOOK
CONFIDENT!!!)

6. Take Green Line at Park Street to Blue
Line to Suffolk Downs. (IMPORTANT:
IF ASKING DIRECTIONS CALL THE
SUBWAY THE T!!!)

7. Arrive at Suffolk Downs and scope the
following: stage door, alternative exits,
possible stakeout locations

8. CONCERT!!!

9. During encore—LEAVE!!!

10. Split up: Jessica and Nora to stage door,
    Peter and Trudy to alternate exits

11. FIND PAUL MCCARTNEY.

# CHAPTER ELEVEN

# Please Mister Postman

Why is it that when you are waiting for something really special, like your birthday or the last day of school or *meeting Paul McCartney*—the days just drag and drag? Even though we managed to get my mother in the car, stretched out on the backseat, for a weekend trip to Cape Cod, and the Beatles Fan Club raised money doing that lemonade stand, and my father prepared for his big trip to Japan— despite all that, it felt like August 18 was never going to arrive.

One really weird thing that happened while I was waiting for August 18, was that Peter started riding his bike to my house practically every day. The first time he did it, I watched him through the blinds, confused. We'd made a plan. Why did he need to see me? He stood on the front steps, I guess trying to decide if he would ring the bell or not. Luckily, he just went away. Until the next day. That time he rang the doorbell. I, of course, ignored it.

"Trudy!" my mother yelled. "Answer the door!"

"It's those guys selling encyclopedias," I told her.

Two guys in black suits really did appear every few months hoping to sell us encyclopedias, even though we already had a set of encyclopedias.

The doorbell rang again.

"Well, tell them we already have a set!" Mom called.

"You told me never to open the door to strangers," I said, stalling.

If I opened the door, would I have to let Peter in?

And then what would I do?

"Oh, for heaven's sake," Mom muttered.

I kind of held my breath, but the doorbell stayed silent. Back at the window, I peeked through the blinds and saw Peter on his bike, heading down the street. The next day I wasn't as fortunate.

\* \* \*

"How are my peonies?" Mom asked me that dreadful afternoon.

"Fine?" I said, because I hadn't noticed her peonies at all.

Mom frowned.

"Pink?" I offered.

"Go check them, Trudy," she said.

I was starting to think that all Mom had to do these days was think up stuff for me to do.

"Check them how?" I asked. "Can you be specific?"

"See if they look healthy," she said. "Make sure they're watered. Oh! And choose the two or three nice ones and cut them so we can put them in that nice round crystal vase."

I groaned. This task was certain to cause me lots of problems.

"Make sure to cut ones that aren't open yet," Mom called after me as I went to fetch the garden scissors.

I hadn't even stepped outside and I was already confused. So I went back into the living room.

"Cut closed peonies?" I said.

Mom had opened *Tai-Pan*, the big fat book she was reading—*If I have to sit here all summer I might as well learn something!* It was about an English guy who wants to turn the island of Hong Kong into a fortress for Britain in the nineteenth century, and once she started reading it, good luck getting her attention.

"Make sure they're hard as marbles," Mom said without looking up. She was lost in China with the book's hero, Dirk Struan.

I got the gardening scissors and went outside on my mission. There they were, the peonies, all pink and feathery. They really were pretty, and I felt confident that I could report to Mom that the peonies were doing just fine. I filled the big green watering can with water from the hose and sprinkled around the peonies and the other flowers, too, just to be safe. Then I stood examining the peonies, trying to decide which two or three I should pick.

That's when Peter showed up on his bike.

There I stood, holding that giant watering can, the front of my T-shirt and shorts wet from all the watering I'd done. I was barefoot, and my feet were kind of dirty from being in the garden. And I hadn't even combed my hair because why bother when all you do is run around taking orders from your mother all day?

"What are you doing here?" I asked him.

"I have important information," Peter said.

ANN HOOD

"About?"

"The Beatles," he said.

"What?"

"Two words," Peter said. "Hotel Somerset."

"Peter, I am out here choosing two or three perfect peonies to bring inside to my invalid mother. Could you just spit it out?"

"That's where they're staying in Boston," he said. "The Hotel Somerset. Corner of Commonwealth Avenue and Charlesgate East."

"Not the Parker House?"

"Nope. The Hotel Somerset."

"Are you a hundred percent sure?"

He grinned. "I am."

He got back on his bike. But he didn't go away.

"Do you know what you're going to say to him?" Peter asked me.

I shook my head. "Not yet. Do you?"

Peter grinned. "Yup."

Before I could say anything more, he was off,

SHE LOVES YOU (YEAH, YEAH, YEAH)

leaving me to figure out how to modify our plan. How were we ever going to get from Suffolk Downs to the Hotel Somerset in time to catch the Beatles before they disappeared inside?

Out of desperation and hope I wrote a bunch of letters to Paul McCartney. Technically, it was six copies of the same letter.

> Dear Paul,
>
> I am the president of the Robert E. Quinn Beatles Fan Club, the oldest Beatles Fan Club in the entire state of Rhode Island. The entire fan club is attending the Beatles concert in Boston on August 18. Would it be possible to meet with you afterward? We won't take up too much of your time—we know how tired you must be after a concert! But if we could take one picture with you and get autographs, we would be most grateful.

*Eagerly awaiting your reply.*

*Your biggest fan,*

*Trudy Mixer*

My brilliant idea was that instead of sending the letters to the general address where every letter to every Beatle went, I could send mine to the stadiums where the Beatles were performing all summer. Who else would get such a brilliant idea? Practically a no-fail idea. I could almost see it, the secretary of the president of the stadium going through his mail, seeing the pale blue envelope addressed to Paul McCartney in perfect penmanship, and handing it to her boss. "A letter for Mr. McCartney, sir," she'd say, and the president of the stadium saying, "I'll give it to him personally."

As I licked each envelope closed and stuck a stamp on it, I felt hopeful. I'd included my address and my phone number so Paul would know how to reach me. Or maybe before he introduced one of the songs during the concert he'd say, "Trudy Mixer, please come backstage after the show."

*International Amphitheatre, Chicago, Illinois*

*Olympia Stadium, Detroit, Michigan*

*Cleveland Stadium, Cleveland, Ohio*

*DC Stadium, Washington, DC*

*John F. Kennedy Stadium, Philadelphia, Pennsylvania*

*Maple Leaf Gardens, Toronto, Canada*

I stacked them up and headed to the mailbox, feeling very excited about the idea that one of them might end up in Paul McCartney's hand. His left hand, I thought, because Paul was a south-paw. I sighed. I knew every single thing about Paul

McCartney. Surely my knowledge and devotion would mean something to the part of the universe that decided who got what.

It was so hot out that the air felt like a wet heavy blanket. I shifted my grip on the letters so my sweat didn't blur the ink. At the mailbox I took a deep breath, almost wishing I had one of Jessica's dumb good-luck charms.

"Here goes," I said, and opened the slot. "Please find your way to Paul McCartney," I whispered as I dropped the letters inside.

"Is that Gertrude Mixer talking to a mailbox?" a familiar, irritating voice said.

I turned to find not just Kim, owner of the voice, but the entire Future Cheerleaders Club standing on the opposite corner. They didn't look hot and miserable like I felt. Instead, they had golden tans and perfect ponytails and clean white Keds without even one scuff mark, and they were all dressed in identical white shorts and cute red T-shirts.

"Trudy," I said, trying to sound like I wasn't a person with dirty feet and sweaty hair and flushed cheeks. "My name is Trudy."

They seemed to all giggle at once.

"Do you think there's a hidden camera in there and you're going to be on *Candid Camera*?" Kim asked with a smirk.

"I'm just mailing letters to Paul McCartney," I said.

They giggled again.

Becky said, "The Beatles are okay, I guess. But the Rolling Stones are so much cooler."

Standing in the middle of the Future Cheerleaders I saw Michelle looking down at her Keds. Was she embarrassed for them? Or for me?

The cheerleaders stared at me and I stared back at them. Until finally Kim started a repeat-after-me song—*Quinn is great and Quinn is good!* And they all answered *Quinn is great and Quinn is good!*—and they marched off down the street.

I still stood there, watching them and telling myself that not one of them was going to meet Paul McCartney. Not one.

"Sound off! One two!" Kim called and they all responded, "One two!"

I felt tears burning my eyes and I had a terrible thought: I was jealous. Of Michelle and Kim and all of those happy clean girls singing their way down the street. All I had was an invalid mother, three oddball friends, a father who didn't know I was alive anymore, and a sliver of hope that meeting Paul McCartney could change all that.

# CHAPTER TWELVE

# Paperback Writer

REVISED OPERATION MEET PAUL MCCARTNEY

THE ROBERT E. QUINN BEATLES FAN CLUB

PLAN B:

August 18, 1966

1. Jessica and Trudy tell parents they
   are having a sleepover at Nora's. Nora
   tells parents she is sleeping over at
   Trudy's. Peter tells parents he is on a
   campout with sixth-grade boys for team
   building.

2. Meet at the RIPTA bus stop in front of

fire station on Providence Street at
1 p.m.

3.  Board 1:15 bus to Providence.
    (IMPORTANT: ACT LIKE YOU DO THIS
    EVERY DAY!!!)

4.  Arrive at bus terminal at 2 p.m. Buy
    tickets for bus to Boston.

5.  Board 3 p.m. bus to Boston,
    arrive 4 p.m. (IMPORTANT: LOOK
    CONFIDENT!!!)

6.  Take Green Line at Park Street to Blue
    Line to Suffolk Downs. (IMPORTANT:
    IF ASKING DIRECTIONS CALL THE
    SUBWAY THE T!!!)

7.  Arrive at Suffolk Downs and scope the
    following: stage door, alternative exits,
    possible stakeout locations

8. CONCERT!!!

9. During encore—LEAVE!!!

10. Take taxi to Hotel Somerset.

11. Split up: Peter and Trudy to kitchen entrance, Jessica and Nora to front entrance

12. FIND PAUL MCCARTNEY!!!

# CHAPTER THIRTEEN

# I Feel Fine

Ten days before the concert and less than a week before Dad left for Japan, he came home whistling a song I'd never heard before. Dad is a very good whistler. Sometimes on long car drives we play Name That Tune, except instead of singing we make Dad whistle and we have to guess the song. For Mom, he always does Frank Sinatra songs. For me, the Beatles. But this one? I had no idea.

"Any guesses, Trudy?" he asked me as he placed his briefcase on the table Mom had put in the entryway for just that reason.

I shook my head no.

Dad was loosening his tie and rolling up his shirtsleeves because we were definitely in the middle of a heat wave.

He started to whistle again. A different song than the first one and another one that I couldn't name. Had Dad become a Rolling Stones fan or something?

"I give up," I mumbled.

He motioned with his chin toward the briefcase. "Open her up," he said.

Opening his briefcase was one of my favorite things to do. I loved how the heavy brass clasps unlocked with a pop and how the smell of leather filtered out as soon as I lifted the lid. Inside there were always neatly stacked folders and papers, pens lined up in a row, and sometimes—like today, I supposed—a treat inside for me: a pack of bubble gum that came with Beatles cards or a macramé bracelet. Even better was when Dad let me polish his wing tips on a Sunday afternoon. I loved laying the newspaper on the kitchen floor and taking out all the supplies: the chamois cloth and bottle of black polish and buffer that made the shoes shiny.

"Go on," Dad was saying.

So I unlocked the heavy brass clasps and lifted the lid. That smell of leather came rushing out and I closed my eyes for an instant and breathed in real deep. When I opened them, I couldn't believe what I saw lying there on top of those colored folders and lined legal pads.

*Revolver.* The Beatles' brand-new album.

Even though he'd forgotten we were supposed to go to Dunkin' Donuts and then to RecordLand together, I didn't really mind. Here, right in front of me, was the new Beatles album.

I'd never seen an album cover like it.

Instead of John, Paul, Ringo, and George staring back at me like they did on their last album, *Yesterday and Today*, or grinning, like on *Beatles VI*, there was just a black-and-white ink drawing of their faces with images of them coming out of their hair.

"It takes some getting used to," Dad said. Then he added, "So do the songs. Peterson and I played it at the office and no one really liked it very much."

"That first one you were whistling was nice," I said, which perked Dad up.

"'Here, There and Everywhere,'" he said, slapping his hands together. "Let's play that one."

He took the album out of his briefcase, and together we walked to his study. I felt so warm and good inside. This was what Dad and I shared! What we both loved! Mom didn't understand. But we did. The Beatles were not only the best group to have ever lived, but they also belonged to Dad and me.

**\* \* \***

*Revolver* only had eleven songs on it, probably because *Yesterday and Today* had just come out a couple months earlier. Still, Dad thought an album should have more songs. "If I'm paying three dollars and forty-nine cents for an album, I think I should get a lot of music, don't you, Trudy?" I guessed he had a point, but eleven new Beatles songs was good enough for me.

Except, they weren't good enough for Dad.

Usually we sat and listened to a new Beatles album tapping our toes and nodding our heads to the beat, smiling the whole time. Dad didn't smile so much as we listened to *Revolver.*

The first song, "Taxman," had him positively frowning. And he actually got up and stopped the record halfway through "Love You To."

"What kind of music is this?" he asked, bewildered.

"Indian? I think?" I said. I'd read that George Harrison had become fascinated with India and an instrument from there called a sitar that made these kinds of high-pitched buzzy sounds.

Dad just shook his head and skipped the rest of

the song, placing the needle precisely in the groove before the next one, which was "Here, There and Everywhere." This made him seem happy again, but then "Yellow Submarine" came on and he stood up again. He didn't stop the song, but he did have that bewildered look on his face again.

"'We all live in a yellow submarine'?" he said, repeating the line from the song. "What does that even mean?"

"It's a story, Dad. About a bunch of friends on a . . . a . . . sea voyage."

Truth was, I didn't really understand it either. In some ways, these songs didn't even sound like *the Beatles*.

"It sounds like a children's song," Dad muttered.

He wasn't much happier with the second side, especially the song "Tomorrow Never Knows."

"This is crap, Trudy," Dad said, which was about the harshest thing he'd ever say. When he got upset he said things like, "Amster*dam*!" or "*H-E*-double hockey sticks!" So calling that song crap was pretty serious. I started to get worried.

"I like 'Good Day Sunshine,'" I offered.

Dad sighed. "Me too," he said.

"Do you know why they called the album *Revolver*?" I asked him. Like me, Dad loved fun facts.

"Because an album turns," I said. "It *revolves*."

Dad smiled a little. "Our boys do love puns, don't they?"

I smiled, too. At least they were still *our boys*.

"Like us," he added.

I was almost relieved that Dad still loved the Beatles, that *Revolver* hadn't ruined everything, when Dad said, "Maybe they peaked with *Rubber Soul* and they're finished."

"No!" I said, because if Dad stopped liking the Beatles, we would have absolutely nothing in common. And then what?

\* \* \*

After dinner—hot dogs and beans, made by Dad

because Mom was too hot and weary from lugging her cast around in the heat—I took *Revolver* over to Theresa's. Even though she drove me crazy, she was responsible for me seeing that first ever Beatles appearance on *The Ed Sullivan Show*. Plus, for once, I had something before she did.

"Hi," she said through the screen door to her kitchen.

I held up the album, expecting her to scream with excitement.

Instead, she said, "I heard it's not very good."

"It's great," I said. "It's the Beatles!"

She opened the door to let me in.

"We had salad for dinner," she said.

"Just salad?"

Theresa nodded. "Mom got the recipe out of *Gourmet* magazine. It's called chef's salad and it has ham and turkey and Swiss cheese and hard-boiled eggs. Perfect for a hot summer night," Theresa added.

I didn't tell her we'd had hot dogs and beans. It sounded so unsophisticated.

"Trudy's here," Theresa called to her mother as we walked past the dark living room. A big fan whirred in the window and an old black-and-white movie was on the television. A plume of smoke rose from Mrs. Mazzoni's cigarette.

"Hi, Mrs. Mazzoni," I said.

"How's your mother's leg?" she asked without turning to look at me.

"It still hurts," I said.

"Send her my kind regards," Mrs. Mazzoni said. "I'll bring over a nice Waldorf salad tomorrow."

Mrs. Mazzoni was obviously in a salad phase.

"Thanks," I said.

"Trudy brought over the new Beatles album," Theresa said. "We're going upstairs to listen to it."

"I heard it's terrible," Mrs. Mazzoni said. "Too psychedelic."

"Oh no. It's really good," I said, even though as

soon as she said the word *psychedelic*, I knew she was right. Like that song Dad hated so much. And that sitar.

Theresa's room was painted bright yellow and she had Peter Max posters on the walls that said *LOVE* in bubble letters or had a big yellow sun shining on hot pink and red flowers. She also had two vinyl beanbag chairs, one yellow and one orange. I had asked my mom if I could get a beanbag chair, but she said they were bad for your back and could ruin your posture. Still, I loved flopping onto Theresa's, feeling the little pellets inside shift around to accommodate me.

That's what I did right off, flop onto the yellow beanbag while Theresa put *Revolver* on the record player.

We didn't say anything while the record played, just sat across from each other on the beanbags. I watched Theresa as she listened, trying to figure out her reaction to the album. But her face didn't betray whatever it was she was thinking, even during "Yellow Submarine" and "She Said She Said."

When the last song finished, Theresa said, "Well, it is kind of psychedelic."

"Kind of," I said. "But not like Frank Zappa or anything."

Theresa agreed. "Or 'Sunshine Superman,'" she said, naming the Donovan song that her mother took away from her because it sounded too psychedelic.

Psychedelic was part of the way the world was changing, and it made me feel nervous. It had something to do with drugs, and hippies, and lots of things I didn't really understand. I liked songs I could sing along with, songs that didn't have back loops and sitars and gongs. Why couldn't the Beatles just keep writing music like that?

# CHAPTER FOURTEEN

# Please Please Me

Here are things that have made me happy:

1. When I was little, maybe three or four, I thought grass was like a big green blanket that had been laid over the earth. Then one day I was playing in the yard and I stooped to pick a dandelion that had gone to puff. You know how the yellow petals turn into grayish white puff? If you make a wish and blow all of that puff off the stem, your wish will come true. That was what I was after: my wish. But instead of picking the

dandelion, excitement seized me. Grass wasn't a blanket at all! Instead it was made up of slender individual blades. I plucked one blade, then another, and another, until I had a bouquet of grass. "Mommy!" I yelled, running back into the house with the grass clutched in my sweaty, dirty hands. "Grass!"

2. Christmas. 1960. I was six; Barbie was one. A year earlier Theresa Mazzoni had come over swinging a skinny doll by its brunette ponytail. The doll was dressed in a zebra print bathing suit with ridiculously small red plastic high heels. All of my dolls looked like babies. Their eyes opened and shut when you picked them up and laid them down. They drank milk from a baby bottle that magically refilled when they finished. One doll, Chatty Cathy, was slightly older than a baby, and when you pulled the chatty ring at the back of her neck she

talked: *I love you. I hurt myself! May I have a cookie?* I had never seen anything like the doll Theresa was wielding that day. "She's Barbie," Theresa said in that superior way she has. For months I begged and whined for a Barbie doll. Finally, the next Christmas, there she was under the tree, dressed in a black-and-white-striped full-skirted dress and black high heels. My Barbie was blond and her hair was shaped into a bubble cut. Santa left four more outfits for her, including an extravagant wedding dress. And a lilac plastic wardrobe to hang her clothes in and keep her tiny shoes in drawers. Barbie.

3. "Today," Mrs. Mellon, my second-grade teacher, announced, "I will present the Good Citizen Award. The Good Citizen Award goes to the student who politely raises their hand and waits to be called on,

does tasks without being asked, follows rules closely, and is always ready to help others." Mrs. Mellon held up a beautiful official certificate with an impressive red seal in the lower right-hand corner. "The Good Citizen Award goes to . . ." Here she paused for a million years. My heart was going crazy against my ribs. An award! With a real seal! Mrs. Mellon smiled her coral lipsticked lips and said: "Trudy Mixer."

4. First sleepover with Michelle. We had pizza and orange soda and popcorn and danced the cha-cha on a big mat with footprints on it that tells you where to step. We stayed up past midnight, which was the first time I'd ever done that. When her mother finally made us go to bed, I climbed into the twin bed across from hers. The sheets and the bedspreads and the curtains in her room are the same purple and white check, and

there's a fuzzy purple rug between the two beds and a white night table with a lamp shaped like a ballerina, and we stretched our arms across that space and held hands until our arms fell asleep and we had to let go.

5. The Beatles on *The Ed Sullivan Show*, February 9, 1964. Of course.

6. Also: The Beatles on *The Ed Sullivan Show*, February 16, 1964.

7. Also: The Beatles on *The Ed Sullivan Show*, February 23, 1964, and September 12, 1965.

8. The first meeting of the Beatles Fan Club. I, Trudy Mixer, stood in front of two dozen other kids and said, "Welcome to the inaugural meeting of the official Robert E. Quinn Beatles Fan Club. I'm the president, Trudy Mixer."

# CHAPTER FIFTEEN

# Love Me Do

Dad and Peterson left for Japan exactly five days before the concert.

The night before he left, Dad packed the big tan suitcase that no one ever used because it was so big and we didn't really ever go anywhere for very long. He also had a garment bag for his suits and shirts so they wouldn't wrinkle on the long flight, and he put his wing tips in shoe bags so they wouldn't scuff. I watched him as he filled his dopp kit with his razor and extra blades, Vitalis and a comb, a toothbrush and toothpaste, soap, a nail clipper, and Old Spice. I watched him, feeling about as sad as I'd ever felt.

Suddenly, Dad stopped throwing stuff in his dopp kit and he looked at me in that way he sometimes did, and he patted the bed for me to come sit close to him and he said, "I'm sorry about the concert, Trudy. Boy, would we have had fun, huh?"

I managed to nod because I was afraid if I opened my mouth I might start to cry.

"I'll bring you back the best souvenir anyone has ever brought back from Japan," he said, and then he wrapped me in a big hug and I could smell that combination of soap and Old Spice and Vitalis that was my dad.

When he let go, I looked right in his eyes, which were dark blue. Mom said they looked like a stormy sky.

"In Japanese, the name 'Japan' is Nippon, which means 'Land of the Rising Sun,'" Dad said.

"Uh-huh."

"It was believed that Japan was the first country

to see the sun rise in the morning," he said. He shook his head slightly, as if to say *How about that?* "Thus the name."

"So you'll see the sun rise before we do and maybe you can send us a good morning when you see it and that good morning will arrive when we wake up."

Dad smiled and shook his head a little. "That's sweet, Trudy," he said. "I will do that. Every morning."

* * *

Peterson arrived to get Dad early the next morning and drive the two of them to New York City, where they would board a Pan Am Clipper at 11:30. It was going to take a million hours to get to Tokyo, but they seemed excited about it anyway. Mom hobbled to the front door to see them off, the two of us standing there and waving.

"Sayonara!" Mom called, which was Japanese for goodbye.

Once Peterson's Ford was gone, it felt dumb to still be standing there, but we were.

"This darn leg," Mom said. "If I hadn't broken it, maybe I'd be going to Japan, Trudy."

"No, you'd be going to the Beatles concert. With me," I reminded her.

"Mount Fuji and cherry blossoms and hot baths," Mom said dreamily. "I've always wanted to see the world, you know."

"You did?" It was funny how much I didn't know about Mom and Dad.

Mom nodded and smiled. "Paris. Rome. Imagine going up the Eiffel Tower or standing in the Colosseum, right where they used to feed people to the lions!"

"That's terrible!" I said.

Mom sighed. "This darn leg," she said again.

"It'll be better in no time," I said, to make her feel better. Parents are full of surprises. Who would have thought Mom, a woman whose idea of doing something daring was making Swedish meatballs, actually dreamed of seeing the world.

"You know, he has to eat raw fish," I said.

I said it so she wouldn't feel so bad, but instead Mom said, "I know! Isn't that sophisticated?"

Mom looked at me hard. Ever since she broke her leg, she hadn't gone to her weekly hairdresser appointment, so her hair was longer than usual, almost past her collarbone, which made her look younger.

"Someday, Trudy, I'll go to Japan. Maybe I'll even see the Taj Mahal. Or the Great Wall."

I watched Mom hobble off, that giant cast clunking along the floor as she did her best on her crutches.

* * *

The next day Jessica called me. Of course when I heard her voice I thought she was going to cancel on me.

But she said, "Want to come over?"

"To your house?" I asked her. I did not want to go to Jessica's house. It was the last thing I wanted to do. It fell into the category of things that reminded me how low I'd sunk these past few months.

"I baked three different kinds of muffins," she said. "Blueberry, banana, and morning glory, which has carrots, apples, walnuts, and coconut."

"Why are you baking muffins when it's like a thousand degrees out?"

"For the Baking merit badge," she said. "We can listen to records, too."

To my utter surprise, I heard myself say, "Okay."

\* \* \*

Jessica lived kind of far from me, in an older development that had big houses with screened-in front porches and lots of oak trees so the yards were nice and shady. The whole time I was walking to her house, I was thinking how nice it was to get out and do something other than wait on Mom all day, even if that something was eating Jessica's muffins.

The house smelled so good, like cinnamon and vanilla, from all the muffins, which were lined up on the counter in little pale-colored paper cups.

"Take as many as you want," Jessica said.

I took one of each because they really looked good and they were still warm.

It was so quiet in her house that I could hear the clock ticking.

"Are you here alone?" I asked, following Jessica out of the kitchen, through the living room with its green plaid sofa, and onto one of those big screened-in porches.

Jessica had brought glasses of milk and extra muffins with her, and she set those down on a white wicker table. Everything out there was white wicker, which made it seem kind of tropical. Lots of plants hung in macramé plant holders from the ceiling, adding to that tropical feeling.

"It's like Hawaii out here," I said.

"It's supposed to look like Nantucket," Jessica said.

"My father's in Japan," I added, though I wasn't sure if he had actually landed there yet.

"Wow," she said, impressed.

We chewed our muffins for a while, then Jessica said, "My mother's resting. She's depressed."

"Oh," I said. I never knew anybody who was depressed, and this seemed both special and scary.

"My brother got drafted," she said. "He went to boot camp for ten weeks in Parris Island and then they sent him straight to Vietnam."

"Stephen is in Vietnam?" I repeated.

I didn't know anybody fighting in the Vietnam War, either. Who knew Jessica had such an exciting life?

"But look what I found," she said. She dug around in her pocket and pulled out a penny, which she held out in her palm for me to see.

"It's from the year I was born," she explained. "That's good luck."

I thought about all of her good-luck charms that

she'd talked about for months and months. Now I understood. She was looking for good-luck signs that Stephen was safe.

"I've heard that," I said.

"Want to hear the *Help!* album?" Jessica asked.

"Sure," I said.

She went over to another wicker table, this one with a portable record player on it, and put on *Help!* She skipped a bunch of songs and set the needle on "Ticket to Ride." By the time the song was half over, we were standing side by side, holding muffins up to our mouths like microphones, and singing, *"She's got a ticket to ride, But she don't care . . ."*

Boy, did it feel good to be doing friend things again.

# CHAPTER SIXTEEN

# Michelle

Three days before the concert, a surprising thing happened. Mom was going through the mail with one hand and scratching inside her cast with a knitting needle with the other one. That cast was looking pretty ragged, and it had started to smell like rotten peaches. Lately, I preferred to sit across the room from Mom instead of beside her. Which was exactly what I was doing, sitting in the over-stuffed armchair with its pattern of butterflies and flowers that Dad usually sat in, and watching my favorite game show, *The Hollywood Squares*, when Mom said, "For you," and held out a postcard.

I was not a person who got mail, except for official Beatles Fan Club stuff, so this was surprising, even thrilling.

"Toss it over here," I said, holding out my hands to catch it. It was unbearably hot and the stink of that cast was just too much.

Maybe Mom realized that because she did throw the card my way Frisbee style.

On the front was a picture of a beautiful beach with palm trees and big crashing waves. When I turned it over I immediately recognized Michelle's handwriting.

> *Hola! Which is Spanish for hello! Acapulco is really beautiful. Wish you were here.*
> *Luv, Michelle*

Looking at that postcard made me miserable, but I couldn't stop myself from examining the picture again and then analyzing the message. Did she really wish I were there? Instead of Kim? Why had she signed *luv* instead of *love*? To be cool? Or to let me know our friendship had been downgraded? To me, there was a difference between *luv* and *love*. *Luv* was casual and fun and not as important as *love*. And I knew Michelle knew that, too. I considered ripping it up. I considered tucking it into the corner of the mirror on my bureau. I considered crying.

But then the doorbell rang.

Still holding the postcard, I went to answer it, walking through the stifling hot rooms to the front door, where, on the other side of the screen door, stood Nora.

"I was in the neighborhood," she said right away.

Nora did kind of live in my neighborhood, over where some new houses were built. Hers was a low white one that my mother called a bungalow. Apparently, they had a sunken living room that three stone steps led into and a color television and a wet bar. Mom had been there once when Nora's mother held a women's consciousness-raising workshop and reported this to me when she got home. I'd asked her what a women's consciousness-raising workshop was, and she held up a book called *The Feminine Mystique*, which Nora's mother had handed out at the end of the night and told everyone it was imperative that every woman read it.

"She had some interesting ideas," Mom said, "but at one point she wanted us all to take off our bras and burn them in the fireplace."

"What?" I said, noting that Mom appeared to still be wearing her bra.

"A few of the ladies did it," Mom said.

The book was scarlet with big white letters, each word with its own black shadow. I opened it and read out loud: *"Each suburban wife struggles with it alone. As she made the beds, shopped for groceries, matched slipcover material, ate peanut butter sandwiches with her children, chauffeured*

*Cub Scouts and Brownies, lay beside her husband at night—she was afraid to ask even of herself the silent question—'Is this all?'"*

I looked at Mom. "Do you feel this way?"

She sighed. "No," she said, "but some of the women there tonight do. Well," she added, in her I'm-done-with-this-conversation voice, "she did make a very good ham salad. I asked for her recipe and she said the secret was sweet gherkins."

I didn't see Nora's mother around very much, but after that night I did notice that she didn't wear a bra and she also had stopped shaving under her arms.

Thinking all this with Nora standing right in front of me, a wave of pity for her swept over me.

"Come on in," I said, and opened the door for her.

✳ ✳ ✳

Nora and I went and sat in the backyard at the picnic table. I brought my transistor radio and turned on WPRO, hoping they would do a Beatles

Blitz, which was when they played five songs in a row by the Beatles.

"It's ninety-eight degrees in Providence," the DJ said, "so the Lovin' Spoonful sure have it right."

The opening chords of "Summer in the City" came on.

"I like this one," Nora said.

"Me too," I said.

Bees buzzed around us, providing the only noise other than the music. Nora and I had absolutely nothing to say to each other.

"Only three more days," she said after a while, in a whisper.

"I cannot wait!" I whispered back.

We were quiet through "Sunshine Superman" and "See You in September." When "Strangers in the Night" by Frank Sinatra came on we both groaned.

Nora sang along in an exaggerated lounge singer way that made me laugh. I never knew how funny she was.

"I guess I'd better go home," she said when the news came on. "My mother will worry about me if I'm gone too long."

"Does she still have that women's consciousness-raising workshop?"

She looked embarrassed, and I couldn't blame her. A bunch of women eating ham salad and burning their bras in your sunken living room was embarrassing.

Nora shrugged. "I guess so."

"My mom went once," I said.

Nora just stood there awkwardly.

"She said your mom makes good ham salad," I offered.

"Yeah. She puts pickles in it," Nora said. "Well, bye."

She walked off kind of quick, her head down.

Of course as soon as she left the DJ shouted, "Beatles Blitz!" and "Paperback Writer" came on.

"Hey, Nora!" I called after her. "Come back! It's a

Beatles Blitz!" There was nothing like listening to a Beatles Blitz with your friend. But she didn't come back. I guess she hadn't heard me.

"First of five!" the DJ announced as the Beatles sang, *Dear Sir or Madam, will you read my book . . .*

I sat back down at the picnic table and let the Beatles' music fill me up.

\* \* \*

Mom had finished *Tai-Pan* and now she was reading a book called *Up the Down Staircase*, which was about an idealistic teacher in a big-city school.

"So much stands in the way of teachers trying to teach," Mom said when I brought her breakfast the next morning. "You should read this book, Trudy. It's an eye-opener."

The *Today Show* was on and Hugh Downs was reading a weather summary in front of a big map of the United States. New England was colored in bright red. For hot, hot, hot. The smell coming from Mom's cast filled the room, gagging me slightly.

"I am going to melt," I told her, trying to breathe through my mouth. Dad said that was the best way to not smell stinky stuff.

"Try having one of these things on," Mom said. She stuck a knitting needle down her cast and scratched away. "Have you noticed it's starting to smell bad?"

"Uh, yeah. Like days ago," I said.

"When does Michelle get back?" Mom asked.

"I don't know," I admitted.

"I hope you two didn't have a fight," Mom said, narrowing her eyes at me. "You girls have been friends for too long to throw it away."

"We didn't fight," I said, and I could hear the whine creeping into my voice. "She dumped me and the whole fan club for Future Cheerleaders."

"Trudy," Mom said, returning to *Up the Down Staircase*, "I'm sure that isn't true."

"Yes it is!" I said.

Mom peeked at me over the book.

"Why don't you go to Nora's house, then? She stopped by here yesterday, so today you could go there," Mom said.

"I don't like Nora," I said, which wasn't exactly true. I kind of did like her, and Jessica, too. They just weren't Michelle. I thought of that postcard from Acapulco, which I had tucked into the corner of my mirror. Didn't it mean that she'd thought about me, even though she was in Acapulco? But I knew somewhere deep down that she didn't wish I was there with her, not really. That was just what people wrote on postcards. Hot tears sprung into my eyes and I wiped them away with the back of my sweaty hand.

"No one's that bad, Trudy," Mom said. "Everyone has redeemable qualities."

I rolled my eyes.

"I think they have air-conditioning," Mom said.

Even I had to admit that was a redeemable quality.

**\* \* \***

On the walk over to Nora's, the air was so hot and sticky, it felt like moving through cotton candy. If I paused, I could actually see the air ripple slightly, like it does in the desert. But the thought of air-conditioning kept me moving.

The street of new houses where Nora lived didn't have any trees because they'd all been cut down to build the houses. So it was even hotter walking there, the tar all soft and sticky and the sun so bright it made my eyes hurt. Her house was the next-to-last one, which meant I had to walk all the way down that scorching street, but I did get the pleasure of a sprinkler on her neighbor's front lawn spraying me with water when I passed by.

Big wide stone steps curved their way up to Nora's front door. By the time I rang the doorbell I was hotter and sweatier than I'd been all summer. I quick-smelled under my arms to be sure I didn't stink, then I stood still as a statue, waiting for someone to answer.

It took practically forever and I was considering leaving but then Nora opened the door with, yes, a blast of cool air.

"Hi," I said.

She did not look happy to see me.

"Two more days," I whispered, hoping to remind her we were in a big conspiracy together.

"I know," Nora said. "See you then."

And just like that she closed the door.

I could hardly believe it. Was it possible that Nora didn't like *me*? I rang the doorbell again, but this time she didn't even bother to answer. If I could have ripped up her ticket to the concert, I would have. I would have kicked her out of the fan club, too. But the fan club was dangerously close to getting shut down for low enrollment already, and I needed her to help execute my plan to meet Paul McCartney. So all I could do was turn around and make my slow hot way back home.

# CHAPTER SEVENTEEN

# We Can Work It Out

TUESDAY, AUGUST 16, 1966

8 P.M.

OFFICIAL COUNTDOWN TO MEETING

PAUL MCCARTNEY BEGINS:

48 HOURS AND COUNTING

"Why are you so antsy, Trudy?" Mom said. "You barely paid attention to that show you like."

That show I liked was *The Girl from U.N.C.L.E.* in which special agent April Dancer fights THRUSH and other enemy agents. But even April Dancer couldn't distract me from my upcoming plot and the anticipation of looking in Paul McCartney's eyes.

"If you're going to wiggle around like that, make yourself useful and pop us some popcorn. *Houdini*'s on Tuesday Night at the Movies tonight, and you know how much I like Tony Curtis," Mom said.

I did make some Jiffy Pop, scorching some of it like I always did. Then I tried to concentrate on Tony Curtis doing more and more difficult escapes. But honestly, how could I? At this very moment, the Beatles were in Philadelphia finishing their concert. For all I knew, someone at the John F. Kennedy Stadium handed Paul my letter and he knew that I, Trudy Mixer, president of the Robert E. Quinn Beatles Fan Club, was going to be in Boston in just forty-eight hours.

*WEDNESDAY, AUGUST 17, 1966*

*8 A.M.*

*OFFICIAL COUNTDOWN TO MEETING*
*PAUL MCCARTNEY BEGINS:*
*36 HOURS AND COUNTING*

"What in the world is wrong with you, Trudy?" Mom asked me. "Why are you up so early? It's summer vacation! You're supposed to sleep in."

How could I tell Mom that I had hardly slept at all? And that when I did, I dreamed of crowds and buses and running down Boston streets? Suddenly, our plan seemed full of holes. I hadn't ever done any of the things I'd told the fan club I'd done— riding the bus to Boston or the subway anywhere at all. In just thirty-six hours, I had to actually do all that stuff. One missed bus, one wrong subway, and not only wouldn't I meet Paul McCartney, but I also wouldn't even get to the concert.

There was only one person who could help me: Penelope.

Penelope lived in one of the mill houses near the

river, which was a pretty long walk. But I needed to go over the details of transportation with her or I might mess up everything tomorrow night.

"I'm going for a walk," I mumbled.

"But you haven't even had breakfast," Mom said.

"I'm not hungry," I said, and stepped out into the hot muggy morning.

\* \* \*

My little town used to be a thriving mill town back in the nineteenth and early twentieth centuries. Most of the mills had closed by now, but they still stood there like big stone castles over the Pawtuxet River. People who used to work in them could live in houses the factory owned, having the rent taken right out of their paychecks. The houses were all duplexes—two side-by-side attached houses—that lined blocks near the mills. That's where Penelope lived, right up the street from the Royal Mill where Fruit of the Loom underwear used to be made.

On my way to her house, I passed a Dunkin'

Donuts, so I stopped there and got two glazed doughnuts for us. I mean, if you're going to show up at someone's house before nine o'clock in the morning, you should bring something like glazed doughnuts.

Penelope looked sleepy and confused when she opened the door and found me standing there sweating.

"Gertrude?" she said, like she was taking a reality check.

I held up the Dunkin' Donuts bag.

"Breakfast," I said, which made her look even more confused.

Penelope had on cutoff jeans and a faded University of Rhode Island T-shirt with sweat marks under the arms.

"Thanks?" she said.

We looked at each other for a moment and then she said, "Oh," and let me inside.

The house was stifling hot, like there was no air

inside it, and I could smell the faint scent of gas. Penelope's mom was sitting at the kitchen table drinking an iced coffee and smoking a cigarette.

"This is Gertrude," Penelope said. "She brought breakfast."

Of course I immediately felt bad because I'd only brought two doughnuts, but Penelope's mom didn't seem to care.

"Hot out there," she said as Penelope placed the glazed doughnuts on a plate.

"Hot in here," Penelope said.

There was a fan in the window, but it just pushed around the hot air.

"John Ghiorse says we're breaking the record for an August heat wave set in 1949," Penelope's mom said. "No end in sight," she added, shaking her head and stubbing out her cigarette.

John Ghiorse was the Channel 10 weatherman, the only real meteorologist in New England, so everyone trusted him.

Penelope was happily eating a doughnut, her lips sparkling with sugar.

"Dog days of August," she said.

"Interesting fact," I said. "'Dog days' actually means the position of Sirius, the dog star, in the heavens. Not that dogs get super hot."

That was the kind of thing I knew from my father, one of the arcane facts he recited at the dinner table before disappearing into his newspaper.

But Penelope's mom didn't seem impressed. She seemed suspicious.

"John Ghiorse say that?" she asked, her eyes narrowed.

"My father read it somewhere," I explained.

Penelope was working her way through the second doughnut. My stomach growled. Her mother got up, turned on the gas on the stove, and lit a cigarette in the flame.

"Why don't you take your friend to your room?" she said. "I've got to make some calls."

"Okay," Penelope said. "But prepare yourself, Gertrude. It's even hotter up there."

I followed Penelope up a steep staircase to the second floor, which looked like an attic with its sloping ceilings and exposed rafters. Penelope's room was right at the top of the stairs, and instead of a door she had a curtain of beads that we had to part to enter. In other words, it was the coolest, most exotic room I'd ever seen. Inside, there was an Indian-print bedspread hanging from the ceiling, and the lightbulb in the light by her bed was pink, casting a lovely glow into the room.

"So," I said, sitting on the edge of her rumpled bed. Penelope had flopped onto the Pepto-Bismol pink faux leather beanbag chair. I noted that almost everyone in the entire world had a beanbag chair except me. "I wondered if you could walk me through some of the details of tomorrow?"

Penelope blinked. "Tomorrow?"

"Getting to the concert."

"Oh, it's so easy," she said. "Everything's marked really clearly, like the subway lines and where the buses are. You just have to kind of look at the signs."

"Okay," I said. Could it really be as easy as that? Just follow signs?

"I've done it so many times," Penelope said.

I frowned. Those words sounded eerily familiar.

"It's so easy," she said again.

That was exactly what I'd told the fan club. And I had never ever taken a bus anywhere by myself, never mind all the way to Boston and then got on a subway. Sweat trickled down my ribs and back. I tried to read Penelope's face, to see if she was making it up, like I had. But she just looked back at me, blank. In that instant, I understood that it was entirely possible there was no high-school boy, no tickets to the Beatles concert, no nothing. Just a girl like me with big hopes and impossible dreams.

*WEDNESDAY, AUGUST 17, 1966*
*3 P.M.*
*OFFICIAL COUNTDOWN TO MEETING*
*PAUL MCCARTNEY BEGINS:*
*29 HOURS AND COUNTING*

You know how when you feel nervous and worried and excited all at once every single thing that happens makes you feel even more nervous and more worried and more excited? That was exactly what the day was like after I left Penelope's. Back at home, Mom's cast was stinking bad and John Ghiorse was telling people to stay inside because it was so hot and polluted outside. I kept going over our plan with all the buses to catch and subways to find and my crazy idea that somehow— somehow—I would actually meet Paul McCartney, and my even crazier idea that if I did my life at school would get better, and my even more crazy idea that my father would realize that I was special again. He would start paying attention to me. He would remember that I'm more important than semiconductors and Peterson and his big new promotion.

And then who should show up on his dumb bicycle but Peter? He was wearing baggy madras shorts and orange rubber flip-flops and he just looked like the goofiest person on the planet. Plus, there was something weird sticking out of the wire basket on his bike. It wasn't until he pulled up right in front of me that I saw what it was: a ukulele.

Let me be perfectly clear. Playing the guitar, especially an acoustic guitar, is maybe the coolest thing anyone could do. Playing a ukulele? The complete opposite. The most uncool thing ever. If you played a guitar, you might perform in coffeehouses. You might sing folk songs, like my favorite one, "Today," which the New Christy Minstrels sang. It even makes my mother sigh and look dreamy. However, if you play the ukulele, people laugh at you. You remind them of Tiny Tim, the worst performer on television with his creepy wavy long hair and the stupid basket he carries around and the way he sings songs like "On the Good Ship Lollipop" in a falsetto.

All of this ran through my mind as Peter hopped off his bike, kicked his kickstand down, and lifted the ukulele out of the basket.

"I need to show you something," he said.

Yup. It was that kind of a day.

Peter cleared his throat.

And then he started to strum that ukulele.

And then he started to sing.

*"If you knew I loved you, would you turn and walk away? Or would your heart urge you to stay?"*

I had never heard this particular song, and I had to admit that the ukulele didn't sound as awful as when Tiny Tim played his. Also, Peter's voice, though kind of thin, wasn't exactly terrible.

*"These are the thoughts I think, when I see you*

*each day . . . Might your heart . . . might your heart . . . urge you to stay?"* Peter sang. Then he strummed a kind of little musical finale, and stared at me.

I didn't know what to say, so I didn't say anything.

Imagine a boy with a cowlick and orange rubber flip-flops and baggy madras shorts holding a ukulele. What was a person supposed to say?

Peter looked crestfallen, but I wasn't sure why.

"That was better than Tiny Tim," I finally said.

Now he looked horrified. He dropped the ukulele into the basket, unkicked the kickstand, got on his bike, and pedaled away.

THURSDAY, AUGUST 18, 1966

8 A.M.

OFFICIAL COUNTDOWN TO MEETING

PAUL MCCARTNEY BEGINS:

12 HOURS AND COUNTING

I woke up and I had one thought: The day has finally arrived.

ANN HOOD

Just like that, all my worry and anxiety from the day before vanished. In twelve hours, I was going to see the Beatles.

Somehow I got through the morning, even though my stomach was so full of butterflies I actually wondered if I opened my mouth would hundreds of them fly out? I had picked out an outfit, but I kept changing my mind and trying on other ones. Finally, I settled on my miniest minidress, which was covered with a pattern of sunflowers. Mom made me stand on a chair and put my arms straight by my sides to be sure the end of my fingertips met the hem of the dress. Anything shorter was not allowed. I'd grown a little since we bought the dress back in June, so I hoped she wouldn't measure again. I wished I had a white floppy hat like I saw in *Seventeen* magazine, but it was too late for that now. I set my hair with empty Campbell soup cans like *Seventeen* magazine said to do to make it as straight as possible and tried not to imagine how Good Night Slicker lipstick would look perfect.

"Why are you all dressed up?" Mom said when I floated into the living room. Really. I was so excited I felt like I was floating again. I missed this feeling. It wouldn't surprise me if I glanced down and saw that my feet were actually not touching the floor.

"Sleepover," I said. "I *told* you."

"That's right. Nora's. Lucky you, sleeping in air-conditioning."

"Remember, I told Mrs. Lombardi, and she's going to bring you dinner and visit," I reminded her.

Mrs. Lombardi was our ancient neighbor, always complaining about how old she was, and how much her legs hurt, and how she had no one to cook for anymore. Poor Mom would have to listen to all of the complaining, but she'd get lasagna or chicken parmesan or maybe both.

"Oh dear," Mom said. "I'll never be able to get rid of her."

I floated back out of the room to take the soup cans out. Sure enough, my hair fell perfectly straight. I smiled at my reflection in the bathroom mirror.

"My name is Trudy Mixer," I said softly. "Pleased to meet you, Paul McCartney."

THURSDAY, AUGUST 18, 1966

12:45 P.M.

OFFICIAL COUNTDOWN TO MEETING

PAUL MCCARTNEY BEGINS:

PLAN GETS SET INTO MOTION

CHAPTER EIGHTEEN

# Nowhere Man

We stepped off the local bus into chaos. Announcements crackled over a loudspeaker and people rushed past us, fast, with briefcases and shopping bags and hats and high heels and a swirl of perfume and aftershave.

"Now what?" Nora said.

For some reason, she had gotten her hair cut into bangs again and she looked even more ridiculous than usual. The bangs were too short and uneven, which didn't help her overall look, which was, as Mom would say, untidy. Also, she'd worn jeans, even though it was a million degrees. The jeans had ripped at the knees, and she'd sewn a red felt heart onto each knee. "My mom thought they were cute," she'd told us when we were waiting for the first bus. They weren't.

"Trudy?" Nora was asking, and although she said *Trudy* her voice was actually saying *Help*.

"Now we get the bus to Boston," I said with fake confidence.

Peter pointed to a board that hung from the ceiling.

"Boston. Three p.m. Gate three," he said.

At times like this, I wanted to hug him.

"Right," I said. "Gate three."

I went to buy the tickets while they went to get in line. The lady at the ticket counter frowned at me.

"You going to Boston alone?" she asked me.

"Oh no! I'm going with the Beatles Fan Club!" I smiled at her, showing all my teeth.

"Really?" she said, impressed. "You going to the concert tonight?"

I nodded.

"Now that is something you will remember for the rest of your life," she said, sliding four round-trip tickets to Boston toward me. "How about that."

I thanked her and got away, fast, in case she asked me more questions or changed her mind. As I made my way to gate three, I noticed that Penelope was nowhere to be seen. This was definitely the best bus to take to get to the concert on time, and I felt bad that my instinct had been right: Penelope wasn't going to the concert. If I had a fifth ticket, I would have found her somehow right then and given it to her.

Peter, Jessica, and Nora were all looking at me expectantly, so I held up the bus tickets before I even reached them, and such great relief swept over their faces that I waved the tickets in the air and did a little dance, just for effect.

In no time, we were boarding the bus and sitting two by two—Peter and me, Jessica and Nora—across the aisle from each other. I had the sign we'd made at our fan club meeting rolled up and I patted my pocketbook again, just before the bus pulled out of the station, just checking that the tickets were still there. They were. I could feel the points of the corners of the envelope, the slight bump of the four tickets inside.

"Trudy," Peter said softly, "even if we don't actually get to meet Paul McCartney, even if the Beatles don't play any of the songs I want them to play, this is already the best day of my life."

"Mine too," I said.

I looked out the window, watching Providence disappear and the bus cross the border into Massachusetts.

"Trudy?" Peter said again.

"Mmm?" I said, without turning around to look at him.

"Nothing," he said.

That was okay with me. I didn't really feel like

talking. Already the traffic was getting bad, all these cars with all these people moving toward the best day of their lives.

**\* \* \***

If the bus terminal in Providence was bustling and confusing, the one in Boston was a million times worse. So many people rushing about. So many buses groaning into and out of the gates. Announcements and signs and the smell of stale popcorn and stale people. All of it swirling around the four of us as we stood there, paralyzed.

Once again, Peter came to the rescue.

"The T," he said, pointing to a sign, which was in fact the letter *T*.

We all stood still, getting our bearings, catching our breaths, and maybe even patting ourselves on the back. We had made it to Boston. The plan was in place, moving along just as we'd envisioned.

"We want the Green Line," I said, and I started toward it, the others following close behind. This was the trickiest part of our journey. We needed to take the Green Line to Government Center and then transfer to the Blue Line. From there it was seven stops to Suffolk Downs. I'd studied the MBTA map in a book at the library, carefully copying down the stops: State, Aquarium, Maverick, Airport, Wood Island, Orient Heights, Suffolk Downs. I even knew the Blue Line was called Blue because it runs under Boston Harbor, a fact I knew my father would have liked to hear if he wasn't in Japan.

"I've never been on a subway," Nora said, and I wasn't sure if it was fear or excitement that was making her voice shake.

"Neither have I," Jessica said. "This is so cool."

We were swept up in the crowd of people going to the Green Line, carried along with them. I stood in line at the booth to buy our tokens, carefully counting out four dollars and taking the tokens the grumpy man in the booth dropped into the tray. Then we put them in the slot and went through the turnstile, feeling very sophisticated. Or at least, I felt sophisticated. Nora looked pretty terrified. Jessica looked wide-eyed, full of wonder. And Peter . . . well . . . I couldn't read what Peter felt. But as we followed everyone down a ramp and onto the platform, I felt worldly and sophisticated, like a person who rode subways and buses with great ease.

In no time a train pulled up and we crowded onto it. Luckily we all found seats, but not together. Like any city person, I held my purse close to my chest in case of pickpockets working the train. I saw that Nora, who was sitting across the aisle from me, had put her purse down on the floor at her feet, a very dumb thing to do. Anyone could grab it and get off at the next stop. Then what would we do?

"Nora," I called over to her.

The woman next to me frowned. Were subways like libraries? No talking allowed?

"Pick up your bag," I said when Nora looked up.

I showed her how I was clutching mine. But she just stared at me, blank faced.

The train wheezed to a stop. Boylston Street.

I realized I should have written down the Green Line stops too. On the map, Government Center had looked close to Park Street where we got on.

Just like that the train was moving again, and just like that it stopped again. Arlington Street.

"I think our stop is next," I said kind of loud so they could all hear me.

The woman next to me glared.

The train took off and in no time pulled into Copley Station.

A wave of anxiety rolled through me. I thought for sure that Government Center was closer, that our transfer was easy. I'd studied the maps, after all. But mostly the Blue Line.

This time the train seemed to go quite a while before it stopped at Prudential Station.

Four stops and no Blue Line.

"Trudy?" Peter said from somewhere behind me. "How many more stops?"

"I think we're next," I said hopefully.

But the next stop was Symphony Station, not Government Center.

Suddenly, we were stopping and going like crazy. Northeastern University. Museum of Fine Arts. Longwood Medical Area.

"Do you know when Government Center is?" I asked the woman next to me.

She *tsk*ed at me and shook her head. "That's Inbound," she said. "You're going Outbound."

"Outbound?" I repeated. I had no idea what that meant, except that we had done something very wrong.

The woman was standing, gathering her big Jordan Marsh shopping bags.

"Get off here, walk around to the Inbound side, and go back the way you came. Nine stops."

"Nine? The other way?" I gasped.

ANN HOOD

"You need to pay again," she said, *tsk*ing and shaking her head.

I stood, too. "Come on," I told the others. "We went the wrong way."

"What?" Nora said, and it looked like she was about to cry.

"We just have to go back. Nine stops. No problem." I hoped I sounded more confident than I felt. I'd gone from sophisticated to country bumpkin in a matter of minutes. Probably everyone on this train could tell I didn't know what I was doing.

The train stopped. The doors opened.

As I stepped onto the platform, I heard Nora gasp. "Oh, no! Someone stole my purse!"

The train pulled away and all the people who got off rushed toward their own lives. Not the Beatles Fan Club. We just stood there looking at each other, lost and robbed and scared.

# CHAPTER NINETEEN

# You've Got to Hide Your Love Away

Nora wanted to go to the police. But if we did that, I was afraid we'd miss the concert. It was almost six o'clock and we had to backtrack nine whole stops and then transfer to the Blue Line. Our plan was already starting to crumble. If we had to find a policeman and report a theft, who knows how long it would take?

"Was there anything important in there?" Jessica asked Nora.

She looked worried, but I wasn't sure if it was because one of us had been robbed or if, like me, she thought we might not make it to Suffolk Downs on time.

Instead of answering, Nora burst into tears, which made Peter terrified.

"Uh-oh," he said helplessly.

"Did you have a lot of money in there?" I asked Nora, but she only cried harder.

"Do you want me to try to find a policeman?" Jessica asked.

But Nora didn't answer her either. She just kept crying.

Jessica rubbed her back, the way a mother might soothe her baby, except I could tell Jessica felt kind of weird doing it.

Time passed. A lot of time.

I knew this because there was a big clock right in front of us, reminding me how late it was getting.

"Maybe we should just go?" Peter finally said. "I mean, stick with the plan?"

"I think that's a good idea," I said, grateful to him once again.

"Well, if it's okay with Nora," Jessica said hesitantly.

Even though Jessica had a million Girl Scout merit badges that claimed she could do stuff like administer first aid, identify birds, sew, bake, repair a bicycle, do chemistry experiments, knit, babysit, and all sorts of seemingly useful things, when push came to shove—like right now—she honestly had no idea what to do.

"Nora?" I said, trying not to sound impatient. "Should we just go to the concert?"

I swear, that big clock had become my enemy, standing there ticking away the minutes.

Nora's crying had turned into whimpering.

"Are you worried that you're going to get in trouble?" Jessica said.

With that, a whole new torrent of crying began.

"Your mother will understand," I said.

Honestly, I had no idea if her mother would be mad or not. I was just being selfish, trying to calm her down and get us all to the concert.

Nora turned on me, her eyes wild and her voice

sharp. "How do you know what my mother will do? I don't even know."

"If there wasn't anything valuable in there—" I began, but she cut me off.

"Only the most valuable thing I own," Nora said. "The one picture of me with my mother."

This did not make any sense. I knew that Nora and her mother were really close, that she was always running home to be with her or talking about how great she was. But maybe her mother still had the negative for that picture and they could print out a new one. For certain they could take a new one, and that might be even better than the picture that was lost.

Nora wasn't giving me a chance to say any of this logical stuff, she just kept saying, "You have no idea. You have no idea."

Peter started pacing back and forth on the platform. Maybe he was trying to think of a solution. Maybe he was walking off the nervous energy like I had bubbling up inside me. Maybe he just didn't know what to do.

All of a sudden Jessica shouted, "Officer! Officer!"

Sure enough, a Boston policeman was walking past in his navy blue uniform and hat. He was tall with broad shoulders, like a football player. His badge said OFFICER MURPHY.

He strolled over to us, looking kind of amused.

"How can I help?" he asked Jessica.

"We ... I mean ... she has been robbed," Jessica said, pointing to Nora, who was sniffling and crying softly.

"Ah! Were you hurt, miss?" the policeman asked, the amusement replaced now with concern.

Nora shook her head no.

"What was stolen?" he asked.

"My purse," Nora said in a soft pathetic voice.

"Were your life savings in it?" he asked.

Nora shook her head again.

"Did you see who took it?"

"No," Nora squeaked.

"I told her to hold it instead of leaving it on the floor," I said.

"Did you?" he said, narrowing his eyes at me. "Good advice that's not going to help anyone now, is it?"

The policeman kneeled down so that he was eye to eye with Nora.

"The sad truth is you're not going to get that purse of yours back. We have no suspects. No fingerprints. Nothing. You just have to take a deep breath and continue on your way home."

"Oh!" Jessica said. "We're not going home. We're going to see the Beatles."

The policeman looked surprised. "You're taking the T out to Suffolk Downs? You'd better get going then. You've got a ways to travel. You know you need to exit and enter over there," Officer Murphy told us.

I nodded.

"Who's your favorite one?" he asked, already starting to walk away.

"Paul," I said.

"The Cute Beatle," Officer Murphy said with a chuckle. "Me, I like George. He's a deep thinker."

Of course I didn't tell him that no one liked George best. I just half-smiled at him and Jessica, said thank you, and off he went.

"I'm sorry your purse got stolen," Peter said.

Nora looked miserable, but at least she'd stopped crying, which I took as an opportunity to start turning ourselves around. Luckily, everyone else had the same idea, and soon we were pushing through the turnstile, exiting the station, only to reenter on the other side.

"Your mom probably saved the negative of that picture," Jessica said.

"That's what I think, too," I said. "She'll make a new one tomorrow."

To my surprise, Nora burst into tears again.

I looked at Jessica and Jessica looked at Peter and Peter looked at me.

"No she won't," Nora managed in between sobs.

The train arrived, but Nora was crying too hard for us to actually get on it. The doors opened, paused, then closed. Then the train went off without us.

"She can't," Nora said.

"Why not?" I asked, confused.

"Because she's gone," Nora blurted. "Mom left back in January and we haven't heard a word from her since then."

"Left?" Jessica repeated. "Left where?"

"San Francisco," Nora said. "She went there to find herself."

Another train pulled into the station. But this time, too shocked by what Nora had said, none of us could move.

**\* \* \***

There was exactly one kid in the entire school whose parents were divorced. Linda Emmett. Everyone knew that one day, way back in first grade, her father left to pick up milk at the corner store and never came back. It was a tragedy, that's what my mother said. Poor Mrs. Emmett—that's how everyone referred to her—had three kids under the age of six and had to get a job to support them. Linda wore an air of sadness, and embarrassment. Even her house, a little Cape a few streets from ours, looked kind of sad and embarrassed. There was no father to fix the peeling paint or patch the roof, no father to cut the grass or shovel the snow. Poor Mrs. Emmett did her best, but somehow she never caught up with chores and homework and school projects. In elementary school, Linda was always the one whose colonial diorama never got finished and whose book reports were always too short. She had more tardies than any other kid in school.

So when Jessica whispered, "Your parents got divorced?" we all understood how terrible a thing that was.

"No!" Nora said emphatically. "Mom just left."

"Will they get divorced?" Jessica persisted.

But I realized that was beside the point. Your mother leaving was in some ways worse than your parents getting divorced. It meant that Nora's father had to do all the mother things—hair combing, hem darning, bath supervision. That explained why Nora looked so untidy.

"I don't know," Nora was telling us. "I don't know if we'll ever hear from her again."

In third grade, Susan Perry's mother had died suddenly. That morning she'd braided Susan's hair and handed her a lunch of peanut butter and jelly, a banana, and three Oreos. Two hours later the principal rushed into the classroom looking terrified. "Susan," she said, "please collect your things and come with me." We'd all watched Susan as she slowly gathered her books and her pencil case, lifted her green wool coat from its hook, and followed the principal out. At first we thought she was lucky somehow, that something wonderful must have happened. But a few minutes later, the sounds of Susan's sobbing echoed through the school.

No one explained until the next day, when our teacher had us make sympathy cards for her. I hadn't realized that mothers could die at all, never mind so quickly. Of course soon enough I learned that Paul McCartney's mother had died when he was fourteen, and John Lennon's had died when he was seventeen, and I learned how that made them creative and sensitive. But Susan Perry, when she returned to school a week later, seemed exactly the same. Still, her father was known as Poor Mr. Perry, and a year later they moved to Ohio where they had relatives.

Mrs. Perry had died of a brain aneurysm, which

meant a clot in her brain exploded. I was pretty sure if she had a choice, she wouldn't have died. Was Nora's mother leaving on purpose worse? Then I thought about my father, all the way across the world in Japan instead of on his way to the Beatles concert and I thought I might start to cry, too, just from missing him so bad. But at least he was coming home.

"She sent us one postcard," Nora said. "From Haight-Ashbury."

"Where's that?" Jessica said. For some reason she was still whispering.

"San Francisco," I said. "It's where all the hippies are."

"Your mother is a hippie?" Jessica said, her eyes widening.

Hippies, at least as far as we knew, smelled bad, walked barefoot, took drugs, and handed people flowers.

Nora looked like she was about to cry again.

"I don't know," she admitted.

Peter patted her hand. "She'll come back," he said.

"You think so? Really?" Nora said, hopeful.

"Of course," Peter said. "Mothers don't leave their families."

That was a dumb thing to say, since obviously Nora's mother had left them. But it did seem to make Nora feel a little better.

"What did she say on the postcard?" I asked her.

"Just *Peace and Love*," Nora said with a sigh.

"She *is* a hippie," Jessica said.

"She said she was oppressed by the patriarchy and its expectations of women," Nora said.

"What the heck does that mean?" Peter asked.

I actually felt like I knew the answer, but we didn't have time to get into all of that. I thought about the women's group that my mother had gone to at their house. I thought about Betty Friedan and her book. Was she maybe a little right? If

Nora's mother had actually left, didn't that mean something Betty Friedan said made sense?

"What she didn't say," Nora said with a sigh, "was goodbye."

# CHAPTER TWENTY

# Till There Was You

Even though this news of Nora's mother leaving the family and moving to Haight-Ashbury to find herself was confusing and scary, I knew we needed to get moving or our entire plan would be shot. So when Nora said, "Wow, I kind of feel better telling you," I felt hopeful.

"I've been holding that in all this time," Nora said. "And making it sound like my mom was at home. Making it sound like she really cared about me."

I wondered if a mother who left like that could still care about her kid. But we definitely didn't have time to explore that right now.

"I'm glad you told us," Peter said.

"I am, too," I said, surprising myself.

Knowing this made Nora seem less weird. She was just trying to seem normal. She didn't want to be Poor Nora, she just wanted to be Nora. I respected that about her.

I linked my arm in hers, like Dorothy does to the Scarecrow in *The Wizard of Oz*.

"Ready to see the Beatles?" I said.

Nora smiled. "Yes!" she said.

We held on to each other as we hurried down the stairs and onto the train. It felt good to be close to a friend again.

This time I paid super close attention to each stop, and as we approached the station to switch to the Blue Line I called, "This is our stop!" so that no one could make an error.

Our train to Suffolk Downs was crowded with kids going to the concert. I could tell because they were clutching signs or albums or even just by the expectant looks on their faces. It was like all of us were in on something huge and important together, like we were making history.

A girl standing across from me started to sing.

*"There were bells, on a hill, but I never heard them ringing . . ."*

And another girl joined in, *"No, I never heard them at all . . ."*

And a third sang with them, *"Till there was you . . ."*

Then I was singing and Nora was singing, too, our arms linked, our bodies swaying.

When we'd finished "Till There Was You," right away someone began, *"Ooh I need your love, babe . . ."*

The whole subway car, everyone, was singing now, loud and joyous.

*"Ain't got nothin' but love, babe! Eight days a week!"* we ended in unison, our voices raised

together with so much hope and even love that I swear the whole train shook.

\* \* \*

Suffolk Downs was built for horse racing. Peter had wondered if the Beatles would be standing in the dirt of the actual racetrack. I'd told him that was stupid, of course they'd be on a stage, but then he wondered if the stage would be in the dirt. Who cared? Peter, I guess. He was quirky like that. I was starting to realize I liked quirky people. Maybe even more than plain old regular people like Kim and Becky. And Michelle. People were already swarming into Suffolk Downs, throngs of them, giddy girls and even parents who looked like they were excited, too. All twenty-five thousand of us seemed to have arrived at once, and we didn't even have to walk really—we just got pushed along. The building loomed across the parking lot, and we slowly made our way to it.

Even though it was evening, it was still light out

in that way August stays. And it was still hot. And humid. I was practically choking on the smells of Aqua Net hairspray and Dippity-do and too many perfumes and sweat and just hot people.

"Hold on to each other!" I called out to the fan club, but the people around me misunderstood and everyone grabbed everyone else's slippery, sweaty arms. Most importantly, I was holding on to Nora and she was holding on to Jessica and Peter was holding on to me. The worst thing that could happen would be to lose each other because I had all the tickets. I clutched Nora even tighter.

Eventually we were almost at the entrance. I could see the people in red jackets collecting tickets and bright lights beyond the doors. My heart was doing a weird ballet, leaping and jumping and twirling.

All of a sudden, Jessica shouted, "Look!"

She broke free and started pushing her way through the crowd—*in the wrong direction.*

"Jessica!" I shouted. "What are you doing! Get back here!"

But she didn't. She kept moving off in the direction of something I could not see.

"What should we do?" Peter asked me. He must have secretly chewed gum because his breath was all hot and Juicy Fruit smelling.

"We have to go after her!" Nora said. "We can't lose her! In Boston!"

I could still see the tippy top of Jessica's head, but it was getting harder to follow it as she wove her way away from us.

Nora had already started off in the same direction, so Peter and I had no choice but to follow.

"If we miss the concert—" I began, but the crowd was too noisy for any of them to hear me.

It was almost as hard to get out of the crowd as it had been to be part of it. My father had read an article about how salmon actually swim against the stream. That's what I felt like. Except salmon weren't as angry as I was.

Jessica was way across the parking lot, at the very edge of the crowd, standing by a shed.

"Are you crazy?" I said when I finally reached her.

"Look," she said, pointing to the inside wall of the shed.

All I saw were horseshoes lined up there, no doubt to shoe the racehorses.

"We were this close to getting inside and you run all the way over here to look at a bunch of horseshoes?" I said.

Honestly, I felt like when a character in a cartoon gets so mad that steam comes out of its ears. If I were in a cartoon, that would be what was happening.

But Jessica seemed oblivious to the fact that she'd dragged the entire fan club away from the entrance to the Beatles concert, across a hot asphalt parking lot, to a stinky shed to gaze at horseshoes.

"Dunstan," she said all dreamy. "And the horse-shoe."

"Who's Dunstan?" Nora asked, bewildered.

"A long time ago, like around 959, in Ireland, a blacksmith named Dunstan was visited by the devil," Jessica said.

"Are you kidding me?" I said. "Is this one of your stories about luck?"

"The devil had hooved feet, and he demanded that Dunstan make him a horseshoe," Jessica continued, as if I hadn't said anything. "But Dunstan was clever and he nailed a red hot horse-shoe onto the devil's foot, causing him to scream and writhe in pain."

"Jessica," Peter said, "this is interesting but the concert's about to start."

As soon as he said that, music came through the air.

Peter must have seen the horrified look on my face because he said, "Don't worry. That's just

Barry and the Remains, the warm-up group."

"The devil begged Dunstan to remove it, and Dunstan said he would under one condition—"

"Jessica! We have to go!" I said, and I tried tugging her into motion. But she stayed put.

"The devil had to respect the horseshoe forevermore and never enter a house with one hanging above its door," Jessica said.

"Great," I muttered. "Can we please go back now?"

"I need one of those horseshoes," Jessica said matter-of-factly.

Peter seemed to consider this idea. "Wouldn't that be stealing?" he asked after a moment of thinking.

"Hanging a horseshoe facing up, like a *U*, over your door keeps the devil out," Jessica said, as if that explained everything.

First it was four-leaf clovers and lucky pennies. Now, when we were about to see the

Beatles—live!—she had to have a horseshoe.

Jessica started walking right into that shed. True, it wasn't locked or anything, but still we had no business in there and even less business helping ourselves to a horseshoe.

"See how they all have seven nails?" Jessica said over her shoulder because she'd gone right in while the rest of us hovered at the entrance. "Seven is a lucky number."

We all watched her study the horseshoes lined up on the shelf, as if she needed to choose the perfect, luckiest one.

"What if we get arrested?" Nora said, her voice scared and hushed.

"We're not breaking the law," Peter said sensibly. "Jessica is."

"We are aiding and abetting," I pointed out.

Jessica turned around, smiling, a horseshoe in her hand.

"This is really, really a good sign," she said.

"I've been wondering where I could get a horse-shoe. For luck, you know? And I couldn't figure it out because I don't know anybody on a farm or who owns a horse. And just like that, a horseshoe presents itself to me."

"Not exactly," I reminded her. "We were minding our business when you made a beeline over here."

Jessica shook her head. "I need seven lucky things and this is number six," she said.

"Is this for some kind of merit badge?" Peter asked her. "Like a psychic badge or the occult?"

Jessica laughed. "There's no such thing, silly," she said.

She studied that horseshoe like it was the most valuable thing in the world, her hand tracing its curved bottom and smooth iron.

Meanwhile, the crowd inside Suffolk Downs was cheering wildly as Barry and the Remains started their next song.

"We have to go," I said, for the millionth time.

"The show has already started and the Beatles might be up next."

Jessica opened her large bag, the one she'd made for her Embroidery merit badge. Basically she'd embroidered a bunch of red and orange flowers and attached that fabric to an old bag of her mother's. Luckily, the horseshoe fit inside. There was no way we could walk into the concert carrying a stolen horseshoe.

"Okay," Jessica said, all perky. "Let's go!"

We walked all the way back across the parking lot, which had started to grow dark. There was still a line to get inside the arena, but it had thinned. Most people were already in their seats listening to the next warm-up act, Bobby Hebb, who had just started to play.

"See?" Nora said. "The Beatles haven't come on yet, and Jessica has her sixth lucky item."

"Did you say you needed seven?" Peter asked Jessica.

She nodded. "I read this book on how to bring on good luck and it said that if you collect seven lucky items you'll have good luck." Jessica looked at us. "I really need good luck, you guys."

"What's the seventh item?" Nora asked.

"The lock of someone's hair who you love," Jessica said.

"Who's the lucky guy?" I asked.

Jessica grinned. "Paul McCartney, of course."

# CHAPTER TWENTY-ONE

# In My Life

By the time we got inside and made it to our seats, Bobby Hebb was done, and the Cyrkle, yet another warm-up act, was playing. I actually liked one of their songs, "Red Rubber Ball," which WPRO played a lot. If I wasn't (a) waiting for the Beatles to finally come on, and (b) worried that Jessica had scissors in that bag of hers and was going to chop off a lock of Paul's hair, I would have definitely enjoyed them singing that song more than I did. As it was, I just felt nervous.

After the Cyrkle finished, there was an intermission that allowed me to get my bearings. First of all, we were in the middle of a dirt field with the racetracks surrounding us. About a football-field length away stood the rickety stage. They must have built it in a hurry just for tonight. The people on the stage looked tiny because they were so far away and I wondered if we'd be able to even see the Beatles clearly enough to tell one from the other. Of course, I knew who was who just by where they stood. Paul was always on the left, George was always in the middle, and John was always on the right. Ringo was the easiest because he was the drummer. I wanted to see John's long thin nose for myself, and Paul's bedroom eyes, and even Ringo's rings. George didn't have anything in particular that was special, which was one of the reasons he wasn't anyone's favorite Beatle. Still, I'd like to see him, too.

Intermission took about a million years, but eventually the next warm-up group took the stage. All of these warm-up groups seemed like a form of torture, but I had to admit it was kind of exciting to hear the Ronettes, the all-girl band who sang "Be My Baby." They had on short skirts slit up the thigh and big beehive hairdos and lots of mascara and I was relieved that I could see all that if I squinted real hard.

As the Ronettes left the stage, Peter leaned toward me and said in a voice full of awe, "Trudy, the Beatles are next."

Then he did the creepiest thing. He took my hand and squeezed it. Normally I would have recoiled, or maybe even slapped him. But there was something so special about this night that I actually squeezed back before I yanked my hand away. It was kind of like singing on the subway, loud and happy, with all those strangers. Tonight I was doing things I'd never do on any other night.

There was a pause that somehow filled the air with an excited electricity. I guess that was what anticipation felt like. Then, out of nowhere, a black limousine appeared and drove right up to the stage.

The doors flew open and out jumped the Beatles! A shriek so loud went through the crowd that I bet my mother heard it back in Rhode Island. I didn't even realize it at first, but Nora and Jessica and I were part of that shriek, our mouths opened and pure joy spilling out, joining every other girl in Suffolk Downs.

I was grateful that my father had splurged on the most expensive tickets—$5.75! Each!—because even though the seats were set far away, I could kind of see the Beatles. They had on shiny black suits with green collars, and their shaggy mop-top hair. For a second I thought I might actually faint. Luckily, Jessica was grasping my arm, hard, and maybe that's what kept me upright.

John was at the microphone and that voice I first heard on *The Ed Sullivan Show* was suddenly singing one hundred yards away from me.

"Just let me hear some of that rock and roll music . . ."

The only word to describe what happened when John started to sing is *pandemonium*, which was my favorite vocabulary word in fifth grade, and the screaming was so loud I could barely hear the Beatles. People were dancing and jumping and pulling on their hair through the whole song, and they didn't stop for the next thirty minutes, which was how long the Beatles played. Only thirty minutes. But it was the best thirty minutes of my life, from that first song, "Rock and Roll Music," to the very last song, "Long Tall Sally."

In between they sang "Day Tripper" and "Nowhere Man" and "I Feel Fine" and "Paperback Writer" and "Yesterday." How can I describe what it felt like to hear the group you've loved forever singing live, almost like they were singing directly to me, even though there were all those other people there. Imagine if a character you loved in a book, like Jo March or Nancy Drew, suddenly appeared right in front of you, a living breathing person? That's kind of how seeing the Beatles felt, like I'd conjured them up and poof! Here they were.

From time to time I glanced over at Jessica, who was grinning a huge grin, and Nora, who was bouncing up and down in her seat, and Peter, who from time to time glanced over at me. Friends, I thought. And for the first time since April break, I didn't miss Michelle. Not even a little.

Sometimes I could actually hear that famous Lennon-McCartney harmonizing that I listened to over and over again at home on my record player, the harmonizing that my father said was the best in musical history.

As I listened to it, I thought about my father, way far away in Japan, and how he was supposed to be here with me tonight. The Beatles were the only thing that belonged to just us, *and* he was missing them. Would he be impressed that I'd made it to Suffolk Downs on my own? Suddenly, meeting

Paul McCartney became even more important, and it was already really important. But standing there in Suffolk Downs with the Beatles singing "Baby's in Black," I missed my father so much, and my heart ached so bad at how he maybe hadn't thought of me even once since he left, that meeting Paul McCartney became vital. I could picture my father's face when I told him what I'd done.

I didn't have time to get too sad about my dad because all of a sudden, behind the big amplifiers on the stage, a girl appeared. Throughout the whole show so far girls had tried to storm the stage, but security guys kept pushing them back. Not this girl. Somehow she'd gotten up there and now she was making a beeline for ... George Harrison? Who would do that if they had the chance to grab any Beatle? Which was exactly what she was doing. She had George in a hug from behind, and she didn't look like she was going to let go. George looked pretty surprised, and John and Paul were laughing pretty hard, and the crowd was cheering her on because every one of us wished we were the one up there onstage hugging a Beatle. A bunch of guys eventually pulled George from her grip and escorted the girl offstage, but even as the Beatles began their next song I was still dying of jealousy.

Until I remembered:

In less than two hours, I would be face-to-face with Paul McCartney.

\*\*\*

It was about 10:30 when the final chords of "Long Tall Sally" faded away and the Beatles were jumping back into that black limousine. As much as the four of us wanted to stand there basking in the best thirty minutes of our lives, there was no time for that. We had to make our way through 24,996 other Beatles fans, out of Suffolk Downs, and get to the Hotel Somerset before the Beatles did.

This time we couldn't mix up Inbound and Outbound. We couldn't miss our stops or fail to switch from the Blue Line to the Green Line. We couldn't waste time on lost purses or horseshoes. This time we had to do everything exactly right, or we would lose the one-time opportunity in our entire lives to meet Paul McCartney.

I looked each member of the Robert E. Quinn Beatles Fan Club right in the eyes.

"Let's do this," I said with the determination of Agent April Dancer, the *Girl from U.N.C.L.E.*

We linked arms again and pushed our way through the crowd. As we moved forward, I caught a glimpse of auburn hair and heard the tinkling of bells. Penelope Mayer was there after all!

"Penelope!" I called to her, feeling happy and proud at the same time. Happy she did see the concert, and proud that I'd managed to get me and my friends there.

She turned her beautiful face in my direction and smiled.

"Weren't they wonderful, Gertrude?" she said.

"Yes!" I told her. I wished I could say more, compare notes on the concert and everything, but the Beatles Fan Club couldn't stop. Not yet.

*** 

The Hotel Somerset was located at the corner of Commonwealth Avenue and Charlesgate East. It was an enormous imposing stone building with a courtyard in front and, I noticed right away, a lot of entrances.

Even though our plan had been to split up, once we were confronted with the actual hotel, we felt too scared to separate. How would we find each other again? How would we let each other know if we'd spotted a Beatle?

"We should have brought walkie-talkies," Jessica said. "That's what we did for the Orienteering merit badge."

"It's too late for that now," I said, staring up at the hotel facade and the hundreds of windows looking down at us. Some of those windows belonged to the Beatles. Did it make more sense to go inside and try to find them?

"Maybe we should go inside," Peter said, as if he'd read my mind.

"Oh! We could pretend we're room service!" Nora said. "I saw that on the Movie of the Week. These gangsters pretend they're room service and that's how they get in the room of the men they're after. One of them hid on the cart," she added. "Under a tablecloth."

That might have worked on the Movie of the Week, but in real life it sounded like a flimsy plan. First of all, there were probably security men guarding the Beatles' rooms, if not their entire floor. Second of all, how were four kids going to get their hands on a room service cart? Third of all, we didn't know which floor the Beatles were on, and I felt pretty certain that wasn't information hotel clerks gave out freely.

I didn't get a chance to share what a bad idea I

thought the room service ruse was because right then, from around the back of the hotel, a black limousine turned onto Commonwealth Avenue, passing right in front of us.

We all gasped.

Then, under the light of the streetlight, the limousine's interior was illuminated.

It was empty.

The Beatles were already back in the hotel. And our opportunity to meet Paul McCartney had passed.

# CHAPTER TWENTY-TWO

# She Loves You (Yeah, Yeah, Yeah)

We stood in a stunned disappointment, silent.

Until Jessica started to cry.

Of course, I wanted to cry, too. But what good would it do? We'd missed our chance. In a few weeks I'd be back in school, *Ger-trude* Mixer, the girl who hadn't met Paul McCartney. And even if my father was impressed that I'd made it to the concert, I had nothing special to tell him. Some other girl managed to find her way onto the stage and hug George Harrison. Me? I was just the loser who couldn't even meet a Beatle when I was standing right in front of their hotel.

"It's okay," Nora was saying to Jessica. "We got to see them onstage. We got to hear Paul sing 'Yesterday.'"

"That's not enough," Jessica said. "I need a lock of his hair or I'll never see my brother again."

"What?" I asked.

"That's my seventh lucky thing," Jessica said.

She opened that big bag with the embroidered flowers and pulled out a piece of paper. Along the left side was the logo and the name Western Union. I had never seen a telegram before, but it looked like someone had just typed a letter. This one began: *I regret to inform you* . . . and as I skimmed the words I saw Jessica's brother's name.

When I looked up, Jessica was eyeing me.

"He's MIA," she said.

"Missing in Action?" Peter said in a voice that seemed to hope there was another kind of MIA.

"But not everybody who's MIA is dead, you know," she said quickly. "So I thought if I could reverse our family's luck, Stephen would be found alive. I mean, maybe he's a prisoner of war somewhere and he'll escape or get found."

"That makes sense," I said.

In the movies, prisoners of war plan elaborate escapes all the time and succeed.

"Like Steve McQueen in *The Great Escape*," Peter said.

I wished he would stop reading my mind.

"And William Holden in *The Bridge on the River Kwai*," I offered.

"Right!" Jessica said, brightening.

But almost immediately her face fell again.

"Except without a lock of Paul's hair, I don't have my seven lucky items."

"Maybe he'll escape anyway?" Nora suggested.

Suddenly, everything about Jessica made sense to me, all the lucky pennies and four-leaf clovers and even taking that horseshoe. A burst of optimism and bravery surged right through me. If Steve

McQueen and William Holden could escape war prisons, then we could find Paul McCartney.

"Why are we just standing here?" I said. "Let's find the Beatles!"

* * *

An hour later we were still looking. We'd been asked to leave the lobby, twice. We'd tried every door we could find, making our way around that behemoth of a hotel, yanking doorknobs and even trying to climb in a basement window. We stood, defeated, in a side alley underneath the dark starry sky.

"Maybe we should just go home," Jessica said sadly.

I didn't have the heart to tell her that we'd already missed the last bus.

"Look," Peter said softly, pointing up at that big starry sky.

The Milky Way spread out across it, a spray of milky white against the inky night.

ANN HOOD

"See Sagittarius, the archer?" he asked. His fingers traced lines for us that drew a centaur aiming his bow and arrow.

Nora sighed. "I never can make out constellations. Even the easy ones like Orion."

My knowledge of astrology kicked in. Sagittarians, I knew, were idealistic. They aimed high, pointing their arrows at what they wanted and then going after their dreams.

"We can't give up yet," I said, determined anew.

"Trudy, it's hopeless," Jessica said. "The Beatles are all in bed asleep by now."

"Or not," Peter said.

He wasn't looking up at the sky anymore. He was looking down the alley, at the back of a lone figure in a black suit enveloped by a cloud of cigarette smoke. Beneath the streetlight, he looked otherworldly. I blinked, twice, to be sure I was seeing what I thought I was seeing.

I took in the dark shaggy hair, the black suit with

the green—velvet, I realized now—collar.

I gulped.

We all did. Then we all looked at one another.

The Robert E. Quinn Beatles Fan Club had just found Paul McCartney.

*  *  *

Carefully, quietly, practically on tiptoes, we made our way toward him, down the alley. At the corner, he paused, but we kept moving stealthily toward him. He stayed put, also gazing up at the starry sky.

When we were about six feet from him, we heard him sigh softly, and then he slowly turned around.

I don't know who was more surprised. Him, for finding four kids staring at him, or us. Because we had not found Paul McCartney after all.

Looking at us, startled, stood George Harrison.

Now you might think I would be flooded with disappointment in finding George instead of Paul. But to my own amazement, I was gobsmacked. I, Trudy Mixer, was so close to a Beatle I could have hugged him, like that girl onstage did.

I stuck out my hand the way my father had taught me to do when I was introducing myself.

"Trudy Mixer," I said. "President of the Robert E. Quinn Beatles Fan Club."

George looked at me, bemused.

"George Harrison," he said in that Liverpool accent I'd come to love. "Beatle."

We shook hands. Which is to say that I, Trudy Mixer, had officially touched a Beatle.

"Isn't it a little late for you to be out here?" George asked.

"We were just about to give up," Jessica admitted.

"But Trudy said we should keep trying," Peter said. "So we did."

"We had to," Nora said. "We really have to meet Paul McCartney."

I thought George might be insulted, even though he was probably used to things like that.

But instead he just nodded and smiled, showing his beautifully imperfect teeth.

"So it's Paul you came to find, is it?"

"Yes," Nora said. "Not that it isn't great to meet you," she added. "Oh. I'm Nora, by the way."

"Jessica," Jessica said.

"Peter," Peter said.

George shook each of our hands in turn. Then he asked, "Where is this Robert E. Quinn, anyway?"

"Rhode Island," I said. As the president I thought I should be the one to speak up.

"Is that far from here?" George asked.

"Kind of," Jessica said.

"And we've missed the last bus," I said.

"What?" Nora said. "We have?"

I nodded.

"Did you catch the concert?" George asked.

We all nodded.

"It was the greatest thirty minutes of my life," I said. "Until now."

"And why did you come all the way here to meet Paul?" George asked.

I felt like he was asking me, as the spokesperson for the fan club, so I said, "Remember when you were first on *The Ed Sullivan Show*?"

George smiled again. "I do," he said.

"The very next day I started the Beatles Fan Club," I said proudly. "And it was the most popular fan club in the whole school."

"Was it?" George said, also proudly.

"Until this year."

"Oh," George said, and I swear his face fell.

"Future Cheerleaders," Jessica grumbled.

George shook his head. "Seriously? They've displaced us?"

"I thought . . . ," I began, intending to tell him how meeting Paul would immediately elevate me in everyone's eyes back at school. That I would be important again. *Somebody*.

But inexplicably, my eyes stung with tears.

"I thought my father would notice me if I did something grand," I said.

"I thought my mom would come back," Nora said.

"I thought I'd save my brother's life," Jessica said.

"All that from meeting Paul?" George said softly.

Boy, did I love that accent.

"How about you, lad?" George asked Peter.

Peter hesitated, then reached into his pocket and pulled out a folded paper.

"Mr. Harrison," he said, "I've written a song that I think is perfect for the Beatles. And I wanted to give it to Paul McCartney."

"What kind of song? Rock and roll?"

Peter shook his head.

"It's a love song," he said. "For Trudy Mixer."

\* \* \*

On August 18, 1966, I did something grand. I met George Harrison in an alley beside the Hotel

Somerset in Boston, Massachusetts.

But that wasn't even the grand part. The grand part was that I, Trudy Mixer, learned the power of hope, the power of honesty, and the power of friendship. For months I had been upset and embarrassed that the only kids who would hang out with me were the three losers left in the Beatles Fan Club. That night, I realized that every one of us is suffering. Every one of us is dreaming. Every one of us is special.

Even the least favorite Beatle, George Harrison.

How foolish of me to fall for the Cute Beatle and dismiss the others! I knew this that night because George turned out to be sweet and funny and kind. And let's not forget that George is the Beatle who sings lead vocals on one of my all-time favorite Beatles songs, "Do You Want to Know a Secret?"

I remembered that as soon as he leaned down toward me and said, "Listen . . ."

I could almost hear him singing *Listen, do you*

*want to know a secret? Do you promise not to tell?*

But he didn't sing. Instead, he said, "Listen, can you stay right here, Trudy? I've got something I want to give you."

"Sure," I said.

We watched George go back inside through one of the very doors we'd tried to enter.

"What just happened to us?" Jessica said, her voice all trembly.

"Oh, not much. We were just hanging out with GEORGE HARRISON!" I practically screamed.

Then we were all dancing around in a circle. We had actually met a Beatle. And even though it wasn't the Beatle we'd hoped to meet, George Harrison was officially one of the Fab Four.

"Now here's a sight," someone said in that Liverpudlian accent.

Grinning, arms draped around one another, we turned toward it.

There was George again.

And standing next to him was Paul McCartney.

"I hear I've got some pretty big magic to do," Paul said.

My knees buckled a little because Paul was every bit as cute in person as he was on *The Ed Sullivan Show*.

"Which one of you is Trudy Mixer?" Paul said.

That's right. My name, Trudy Mixer, came out of Paul McCartney's mouth.

"Me," I squeaked.

Paul grinned and I tried not to faint.

"Here's fifty signed pictures of me and the boys for your fan club." He winked. "That might get you some new members," he said. "Now what's your dad's name?"

"Charles?"

"Charles," Paul said. He took out a felt pen and signed a picture:

*to Charles Mixer, Your daughter Trudy is the*

*most wonderful bird in America. Take good*

*care of her!*

*Paul McCartney*

That's what he wrote with his left hand, just like all the fan magazines said.

"And where's the bloke that wrote me a song?"

Peter stuttered, "Th-th-that's m-m-me."

"Hand it over then," Paul said.

Peter gave him the song and Paul studied it, humming slightly. "Not bad," he said. "Not bad at all."

Paul looked up, at me.

"Be nice to this boy," he said. "Girls don't get love songs written for them every day, you know."

"Jane Asher does," I reminded him.

Paul laughed. "That she does," he said.

"Mr. McCartney?" Jessica said. "May I?"

To everyone's surprise, she was holding up a pair of scissors. I laughed because Jessica was like

Mary Poppins with that big bag of hers.

"Just a little, okay?" Paul said.

"Just enough to bring my brother home," Jessica said.

Paul looked at her thoughtfully, then exchanged a glance with George.

"Luv," George said—and if you haven't heard someone from Liverpool say that word then you are missing something enormous in your life— "sometimes we pray for help in accepting what comes our way. That takes a bit of magic, too."

I think I fell a little in love with George right then. My own talisman, the autographed picture for my father, suddenly took on new significance. Maybe it wouldn't turn him into the father of my dreams, I thought. And maybe that's what I had to figure out how to live with, just like I had to figure out who I was going to be when school started up again in three weeks.

Jessica snipped Paul's hair, sweeping the locks

into a small plastic bag and securing it with a twisty.

That same big black limousine that had brought them to and from the stage glided up.

"I heard the last bus left a long time ago," Paul said.

And just like that we were shaking hands with Paul and George and climbing into the limo and calling goodbye and thank you.

The limo driver asked, "Where to?" and I gave him my address. By the time we got there it would be dawn. Hopefully I wouldn't be in too much trouble. Hopefully my mother would hobble to the kitchen and make us pancakes.

We drove through the empty streets of Boston in silence, each of us going over our adventure. Each of us, I think, wondering if what had just happened was real, or just the wishful thinking of four friends who needed a bit of magic in their lives. I reached over and took Jessica's hand, and she reached over and took Peter's, and he reached over and took Nora's. It felt good and right to be sitting there like that.

It was August 19, 1966, and the rest of our lives was about to begin.